DAMNATION

TRAVERS AND PALUMBO
BOOK 3

PETER MULRANEY

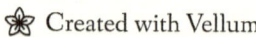

In memory of Gil Haines and the Terka days of our youth.

CHAPTER 1

On a late summer Thursday evening, Alastair Holt, Senior Pastor at Southern Vales Community Church in McLaren Vale, entered his study to write the sermon he planned to deliver on the coming Sunday.

He drew the curtains to close himself off from the outside world and took his seat at the ancient and heavily marked oak table that had served as his desk for over thirty years. As he adjusted the cushion on his chair to the level of comfort he desired, he noticed the stack of unopened mail his wife, Marianne, had propped up against the desk lamp.

He'd made sure, right from the start of their marriage, that Marianne understood she was not to open his mail. In fact, he'd made a point of telling her that although she was his wife, church business was his business, as were letters addressed to him personally. He'd also taken charge of the correspondence addressed to them both, on the understanding he'd keep her informed about anything she needed to know about. In return, he'd promised never to open letters addressed to her personally.

In Alastair's world, wives were submissive to their

husbands, as St Paul had clearly articulated in his letter to the Ephesians, and through his preaching he'd made sure the women in his congregation, including his wife, understood their place. A pastor had to lead his flock by example, according to Alastair's interpretation of the Word of God, and he saw himself as a good shepherd guiding the flock God had gathered around him in Southern Vales.

He picked up the mail and absent-mindedly flipped through the envelopes, dividing anything addressed to Pastor Holt or to the Church from the commercial envelopes containing bank statements and accounts to be paid. There was no personal mail, which didn't surprise him. It all came by email these days.

At the bottom of the pile was an envelope without a stamp, a postage mark, or even an address. The words 'Pastor Holt' were scrawled across the envelope in thick black ink, in a style that reminded him of the pens he'd seen Trump using to sign his name on Executive Orders when he'd been President of the United States.

Intrigued, he picked up his letter opener and slit the envelope open along its shorter edge, before extracting the single piece of folded A4 paper it had enclosed. He unfolded the paper. It was covered in a jumble of different sized letters cut out of a magazine and glued to the page to form words.

It took him a moment to decipher the message the letters spelt out.

NOWHERE IS SAFE FOR YOU PASTOR SCUMBAG - WE KNOW WHERE YOU LIVE.

Below the words was an image of a black and white flag, which Alastair recognised as the flag of ISIS, an organisation he'd condemned more than once.

He scratched his head. He'd seen similar threats posted

as comments under some of the videos on the church's YouTube channel. There must be a local ISIS sympathiser wanting to put the wind up him, he thought, as he crumpled the paper into a ball and dropped it into the wastepaper bin under the table.

He wondered if he should mention it to his son, Thomas, who was also known as Pastor Holt. After all, someone must have hand-delivered it to their letterbox. It was one thing to be threatened online by trolls on the other side of the world hiding behind avatars. They made him laugh, thinking they could scare him into stopping his work of spreading the truth with their hollow threats of meaningless words. But, being threatened by someone local, who actually knew where he lived, that was something, he decided, he probably shouldn't be treating as a laughing matter.

He bent down and retrieved the ball of paper from the wastepaper bin and smoothed it out on the desktop, wondering if it would still hold any clues the police could use to identify whoever had sent it or if he'd obliterated any such evidence by screwing it up and then flattening it out again.

The sound of the garden gate opening and closing caught his attention. It was too early for Marianne to be home from her girls' night out. He wondered who'd be coming at this hour on a Thursday night without ringing first. Even Thomas knew to ring on a Thursday night.

He left the letter on the desk alongside the unopened mail, pushed back his chair, and headed for the front door as the doorbell sounded.

For Marianne, Thursday nights were an escape from the restrictions of her married life. They gave her an opportunity to be herself, instead of always having to be the pastor's wife. Each Thursday night, she did something away from home while Alastair worked on his sermon. It was an arrangement that suited them both. She got to be with her friends and do as she pleased. He got the undisturbed silence he required for crafting his sermons.

On the fourth Thursday of each month, she caught up with her sister, Georgina, and two of their long-time friends, Sarah and Rose, ostensibly to talk about the books they were reading. They met in a local restaurant at seven-thirty, after they'd dutifully served dinner for their husbands, and talked about all things under the sun until the restaurant closed, when they made their way home to their beds.

Although they referred to themselves as the Thursday Night Book Club, they rarely, if ever, talked about books. Tonight, after the usual round of updates on who was doing what and what their children were up to, Marianne was feeling somewhat uneasy as she listened to her friends talk about coercive control as a form of domestic violence, especially the control of a woman's money, a topic which had been getting a fair amount of airtime on the talkback radio shows they listened to.

'Do you have your own bank accounts?' said Georgina. 'There's no way I'd let Malcolm control what I do with my money.'

'I've had my own account ever since I started work,' said Sarah.

'We have a joint account for household expenses and separate accounts for everything else,' said Rose, 'although John earns three times what I do.'

'What about you, Marianne?' said Georgina.

Caught off guard, Marianne blurted out the truth. 'I've never had an account of my own.'

The others exchanged a glance. Marianne felt as though she'd confessed to a crime.

'What about that credit card you use to pay for things?' said Georgina.

'That's linked to Alastair's account,' said Marianne. 'I've never had a job, so I've never needed to open my own account. To be honest, I've never thought about it.'

'Oh, you've had a job alright,' said Georgina. 'It's just that being the pastor's wife is an unpaid position.'

'Do you have to ask Alastair for money?' said Rose.

'Not really,' said Marianne. 'We have a budget. I know how much I can spend on myself each month. In fact, we've had a budget right from when we first got married.' Although, I've never had a say in how it's set, she realised, as she explained herself.

In light of the nature of their conversation, she decided it would be best to keep that insight to herself. She didn't want to be accused of letting Alastair control her.

'Yeah, and if I remember rightly,' said Georgina, 'you were a child bride.'

'I was twenty,' said Marianne, smiling. 'Thought I was all grown up at the time but when I look at the kids today, I'm not so sure I was.'

'None of us were that much older when we got married,' said Rose, 'except for Georgina. She was a veritable old maid at twenty-five.'

Marianne laughed along with the others, relieved at no longer being the focus of attention.

It was nearly eleven when Marianne and Georgina pulled up outside the Holt residence in Georgina's car.

'I'm sorry if I embarrassed you when we were talking about money,' said Georgina. 'Sometimes I don't think before I shoot my mouth off.'

'It's okay,' said Marianne. 'I know a lot of couples don't arrange their finances the way we do. But you know how Alastair is when it comes to family values.'

'Yeah, I often wonder how you put up with it.'

'He's a lot like Dad, you know. Maybe that's why I fell in love with him.'

'That'd be right,' said Georgina, laughing. 'I'm pretty sure Mum's never had her own bank account either.'

'See you Sunday,' said Marianne, opening the door and getting out of the car.

'I'll bring you that book I was telling you about. Perhaps we can talk about it next time.'

Marianne closed the door and stood at the gate, watching her sister's car disappear into the night. When she could no longer see its tail lights, she turned her attention to finding her keys at the bottom of her handbag, before opening the gate and walking up the path to the front door, allowing the gate to swing shut behind her with a clang.

The light in Alastair's study was still on. He must have forgotten to turn it off when he went to bed, she thought. He'd been leaving lights on fairly regularly over the last few weeks, and been a bit defensive when she'd pointed it out to him. She hoped he was only becoming more forgetful, and not showing signs of early onset dementia. He'd only just turned sixty-five, for heaven's sake. Surely God would allow him a few years of peaceful retirement after his lifetime of dedicated service, she thought, as she put her key into the lock and turned it to open the door.

The light in the hallway was on and revealed a sight that made Marianne catch her breath. Alastair was lying flat on his back on the floor, just beyond the reach of the door. Her first thought was he must have had a heart attack like his father, who'd died from one in his early sixties. They'd often discussed the possibility of it being hereditary, despite Alastair's doctor insisting he was as fit as a mallee bull.

Then she saw the small black object sticking out of the centre of his chest, and the pool of blood that had stained his shirt and soaked into the carpet.

For the next few moments, she stood and stared, trying to make sense of the scene in front of her. She certainly hadn't expected to come home and find Alastair, the man who had insisted she live out her marriage vows to love, honour, and obey him to the letter, dead on the floor with a strange black object sticking out of his chest, right where he'd so often told her his heart was.

She took a deep breath and wondered who had killed him, and why. No name or reason came to mind. Everybody in their community talked about Alastair as if he was the living embodiment of the Word of God he was so fond of preaching. As far as she knew, everybody loved him.

She didn't feel angry, like she supposed she should. Instead, she savoured a guilty moment of gratitude for the person who had done him in before she'd given into the temptation to do it herself. Suddenly, she felt exposed, as if anyone watching could read her thoughts. She turned and looked out through the open doorway. There was no-one there. She shut the door, thinking she'd be safer away from prying eyes.

Instinctively, she knew her interests would be better served if she assumed the role of the grieving widow, of the dutiful wife whose loving husband had been cruelly taken from her, no matter what her true feelings about his death might be. Without thinking too deeply, she realised life would be easier for her if people continued to believe what they'd always believed about their pastor, and remained ignorant of things to which only she was privy.

Finally, reality hit her. Alastair was dead on the floor in front of her. She couldn't just leave him there and go to bed. Someone had murdered him. That wasn't right. She had to report it to someone. What if people thought it was her?

She fished out her phone from the depths of her handbag and called her son, Thomas. He was the assistant pastor and lived only a few minutes away in the house next to the church. He'd know what to do, and who to call.

CHAPTER 2

IT WAS four in the morning when Pat and Lina arrived in Galaxy Court, McLaren Vale. The Holt residence wasn't hard to find. A collection of police vehicles in front of a house cordoned off with crime scene tape was hard to miss.

Pat and Lina slipped on their scene of crime suits and presented themselves to the constable who was controlling access to the property.

'Detective Sergeant Travers and Detective Constable Palumbo,' said Pat, presenting his ID.

The constable recorded their details and lifted the tape for them. He didn't need to tell them where the crime scene was located. It was visible from where they stood.

Pat approached the middle-aged woman standing next to the body on the floor just inside the open front door. He didn't recognise her, but her demeanour suggested she was the pathologist.

'DS Travers,' said Pat. 'I'm the investigating officer.'

'Kathy Rice, pathologist,' said the woman. 'Took your time getting here, Sergeant.'

'Bit of a drive from the city, even at this hour of the morning, I'm afraid. What can you tell me?'

'Cause of death is pretty obvious,' said the pathologist, pointing at the black finned object in the victim's chest.

'Looks like some sort of dart.'

'Crossbow bolt would be my guess,' said the pathologist.

'What makes you think that?'

'My husband's a target shooter. He's got one.'

'I thought they were prohibited weapons,' said Pat.

'They are, but there are exemptions for hunters and target shooters. Anyway, we'll know for sure once I get it out.'

I'll need to check on those exemptions if she's right, thought Pat. 'What about time of death?'

'Your victim has been dead for less than twelve hours, judging by the less than complete rigor mortis.'

Pat stepped outside to let the Coroner's men enter the hallway to bag the body and then carry it out to their van. While he was standing on the porch waiting, he noticed Lina leaning up against one of the patrol cars parked in the street. She was talking to a uniformed constable.

The pathologist joined him on the porch with her instrument bag in her hand. 'I'll let you know when I've booked a slot for the post-mortem, Sergeant.'

'Thanks.'

Pat watched her make her way to the gate, then went inside in search of a scene of crime officer.

'Any sign of forced entry, Constable?'

'I'd say the victim probably opened the door, and the

killer let him have it, Sarge, going by the position of the body,' said the constable. 'Look!' He pointed to the white outline of the victim's body on the floor. 'His feet are just outside the sweep of the door.'

'So, it's possible the killer didn't even enter the house?'

'Hard to say, Sarge. According to the responding officers, his wife told them the door was locked when she got home.'

Pat hoped the constable he'd spotted Lina talking to was one of those first responders. 'Anything out of the ordinary inside the house? Any sign of robbery?'

'You'd better take a look at the letter on top of the table in there, Sarge,' said the constable, pointing to the open door behind Pat. 'Looks like our pastor might have pissed off some people big time.'

Pat walked into the room, which had obviously been Pastor Holt's study. A floor to ceiling bookcase filled with books covered the wall opposite the window. Below the window stood a solid wooden table that had seen better times. On top of the table, a bright yellow evidence marker held down a plastic sleeve containing an envelope and a piece of wrinkled paper with cut out letters stuck to it. The envelope was simply addressed to Pastor Holt in thick, black handwritten letters. The paper looked like it had been screwed up and then flattened out again, as if the pastor had had second thoughts about throwing it out.

Pat studied the mess of letters until he'd deciphered the message. Then he snapped a photo of the letter and the envelope with his smartphone, wondering if they'd get any prints from them they could use. He slipped his phone back into his pocket, suspecting they probably wouldn't.

Pat joined Lina in the car. 'What did you learn from the locals?'

'Not much that's going to help us,' said Lina. 'They've spoken to the neighbours on either side and opposite. Nobody saw or heard anything out of the ordinary.'

That's either the truth or they don't want to be involved, thought Pat. 'What about the wife? Didn't she find the body?'

'She hasn't been much help either. Claims she found him dead on the floor behind a locked door when she got home from her girls' night out, at eleven.'

'She didn't ring it in straight away, though, did she?'

'No, that was her son. He was his father's assistant.'

'Admin assistant?'

'No, he's the assistant pastor.'

'So, another Pastor Holt,' said Pat, showing Lina the photograph he'd taken in the victim's study.

'Haven't seen one of those for a while,' said Lina, handing the phone back to Pat. 'Is that an ISIS flag?'

'Think so.'

'Don't they usually post their claims on social media?'

'You're asking me?' said Pat. 'I've got no bloody idea what these ISIS people do. Could be a red herring for all I know. We'll have to get someone from Counter-Terrorism to check it out.'

'We'd better warn this other Pastor Holt in case they're after him as well,' said Lina. 'He lives over on Chalk Hill Road. That's where their church is.'

'Did they say where we could find the wife?'

'She's at her son's place.'

'Guess we'd better go have a word with them.'

CHAPTER 3

LINA TURNED off Chalk Hill Road at the sign marking the entrance into the Southern Vales Community Church. The church building was a solid stone structure that reminded Pat of old churches he'd seen in several country towns in his travels around the state. Going by the appearance of the stonework in the early morning sunlight, he surmised it had been built in the early years of the twentieth century.

In the shadow of the church, behind a well maintained low hedge, stood a modest house of similar construction with a wide front veranda. Lina pulled in behind the white VW Golf in the house's driveway and they got out of the car.

'Thought these community churches were a relatively recent thing,' said Lina. 'This place looks like it's been here forever.'

'A lot of these old churches have had several lives,' said Pat. 'There's probably some other denomination named on the foundation stone. Wouldn't surprise me if this place had started life as a Methodist or Presbyterian church a hundred years ago and closed when those two groups became part of the Uniting Church back in the 1970s.'

'How do you know that stuff?'

Pat laughed. 'My dad was a local history buff. He took me to all sorts of places when I was a kid. Probably even brought me down here to look at this very building.'

'My father brought me down here, too,' said Lina, 'to buy wine.'

'Yeah, we did some of that as well as look at old buildings and cemeteries,' said Pat, reaching for the doorbell button, before stepping back as the door opened to reveal a young man in jeans and a grey T-shirt.

'Pastor Holt?'

'Thomas,' said the young man, offering his hand. 'I take it you're the police.'

'Detective Sergeant Travers and Detective Constable Palumbo,' said Pat, shaking the pastor's hand and wondering about his lack of formality. 'Sorry about the loss of your father, but we'll need to ask you and your mother a few questions.'

'Come in,' said Thomas. 'We've been expecting you. Here, this way.' He stepped aside and directed them into the front room, where a smartly dressed middle-aged woman sat in an armchair with her hands in her lap. 'This is my mother, Marianne Holt.'

Pat did the introductions, then he and Lina sat on the couch opposite Marianne, while Thomas stood behind her. The only other pieces of furniture in the room were a coffee table, littered with newspapers, and a flat screen television mounted on the wall opposite the doorway. Minimalist, thought Pat, as he took in their surroundings.

'I'm sorry about what's happened to your husband, Mrs Holt,' said Pat. 'I hope you're up to answering a few questions.'

Marianne gave Pat a weak smile, a smile that made him wonder what was going on behind the polite facade she was presenting. She looked as if she hadn't slept and was still dressed for a night out, not for a morning sitting at home with her son.

'What is it you want to know, Sergeant?'

'I understand you found the body,' said Pat, feeling a little uncomfortable as she gave him that weak smile again. 'When was the last time you saw your husband alive?'

'It would have been around seven-fifteen last night. That's when my sister arrived to pick me up.'

'And, your sister is?'

'Georgina, Georgina Saddler.'

'Would she have seen your husband when she came to pick you up?'

'You'd have to ask her, Sergeant. She didn't get out of the car, but Alastair came out onto the veranda with me, so I suppose she would have.'

That's something I'll have to check, thought Pat. 'What time was it when you came home and found your husband's body?'

'We got home at ten fifty-seven,' said Marianne. 'I remember seeing the time on the clock in the car as we pulled up.'

'Did your sister come in with you?'

'No, she just dropped me off and then went home.'

'Where were you and your sister between the time she picked you up at seven-fifteen and when she dropped you home?'

'At Vasarelli's.'

'What's that?'

'It's a local restaurant. It's where we meet for our Thursday Night Book Club.'

'Who's we?'

'Georgina and me, Sarah Johanson, and Rose Treloar. We've been friends since we were kids.'

'I'll need their contact details,' said Pat.

'Why?' said Marianne. 'I've got a receipt showing I paid at ten-twenty five.'

Convenient, thought Pat, wondering why she'd even think of mentioning it. 'Do you have it with you?'

Marianne picked up her handbag from beside her armchair, located the receipt and handed it to Pat. He looked at it and then passed it to Lina to photograph.

'We'll still need to talk to your friends and associates as part of our enquiries,' said Pat. 'Standard procedure, I'm afraid.'

'Do you want their details now?' said Marianne, opening her handbag again. 'I've got them here in my phone.'

'If you could give them to Constable Palumbo, that would be helpful, Mrs Holt.'

Pat waited while Marianne took her phone from her handbag and read out the details for Lina to record.

'Now, walk us through what happened when you got home last night, Mrs Holt, if you would.'

Marianne sat on the edge of her seat with her arms crossed. 'The first thing I noticed was the light in Alastair's study was still on. I thought he must have forgotten to switch it off when he went to bed. He's been doing that a bit lately. Then, I let myself into the house and found him lying on the floor. I thought he'd had a heart attack, but then I saw the blood and that thing sticking out of his chest.'

'Did you touch the body?'

'No.'

'Not even to check if he was alive?'

Marianne shook her head and reclined back into her armchair. 'I could see he was dead just by looking at him. He's not the first dead person I've seen, Sergeant. They have a look about them that tells you they're dead.'

They certainly do, thought Pat, especially when they were killed several hours before being discovered, or when you already know they're dead because you killed them.

'What did you do then?'

'I remember shutting the door. I didn't feel safe with it being open. Funny what occurs to you, isn't it?' She looked straight at Pat and smiled again. 'Then I called Thomas. I knew he'd know what to do.'

'Was the door locked when you got home?' said Pat.

'I had to use my key to get in,' said Marianne.

'What did you do while you waited for Thomas to arrive?'

'I sat in Alastair's study. The light was on in there.'

'Did you see anything out of place in your husband's study while you were in there waiting?'

'Not out of place, Sergeant, but there was a strange letter on his desk. It looked like Alastair had screwed it up and then changed his mind about throwing it out.'

'Had he received any other letters like that?'

'I wouldn't know, to be honest.' Marianne looked down at her hands. 'I don't read his mail and he never mentioned it.'

'What about envelopes addressed like this one?' Pat showed her the photo he'd taken in her husband's study.

'I collect the mail every day and put it on his desk after

the postie has been. Yesterday was the first time I'd seen an envelope addressed like that.'

'Did you think it was strange getting something like that in your letterbox?'

Marianne shook her head. 'People often slip notes to Alastair into our letterbox. I thought it was probably something from one of our older members, someone who writes with one of those big pens.'

'How long did you have to wait until your son arrived?'

Marianne turned her head to look at Thomas.

'I got there at around eleven-twenty,' said Thomas. 'I'd just gone to bed when Mum called.'

That tallied with what Pat knew about the time of the call Thomas had made to triple zero. 'And, where were you between seven-fifteen and eleven last night, Mr Holt?'

'What? You think I killed my father?'

Pat smiled. 'It's too early for me to think anything, Mr Holt, but I do need to know where you were last night.'

'I was here, in my workshop. I make toys out of recycled materials.'

'Anybody with you?'

'No, I was on my own.'

'Where is this workshop?' said Pat.

'I use the garage. It's in the backyard at the end of the driveway.'

'He's been doing things in that workshop since he was a boy,' said Marianne. 'He's very good with his hands.'

'It's how I support myself when there's no work going in the vineyards,' said Thomas. 'An assistant pastor in a church like ours isn't paid enough to live on, despite what you might have heard. Southern Vales is not a megachurch.'

'So, why did you take it on?' said Pat.

'Dad was getting ready to retire and wanted me to take over when he did.'

'Did your father make those decisions on his own or is there some sort of board that oversees the church?'

'There's a Council of Elders,' said Thomas. 'They appointed me on Dad's recommendation. The first two years were probationary under Dad's mentorship.'

'Has your probation finished?'

'Last year, just before Christmas.'

Pat turned to Marianne. 'Did your husband work outside the church as well?'

'In the early years,' said Marianne, 'he worked as the groundsman at the Primary School until the community was big enough to afford to pay him a decent salary, and after that he worked in some of the local vineyards when we needed extra money.'

'Do you work, Mrs Holt?'

'Alastair wouldn't hear of it, Sergeant. My job was to be the face of the church during the week when he couldn't be here.'

Pat looked around the room. 'So, this would have been your home before you moved to where you live now?'

'We moved to Galaxy Court last year, Sergeant. Alastair was planning to retire at the end of the year.'

Pat leant forward in his seat. 'You mentioned you saw the letter threatening your husband, Mrs Holt. Do you have any idea who may have wanted to kill him?'

Marianne shook her head. 'Alastair was a good man, Sergeant. He devoted his life to God.'

'What about you, Mr Holt?'

'Dad could be pretty forthright in some of his opinions, Sergeant. I guess he could have upset any number of people.'

He looked at his mother with an expression that made Pat think he was expecting her to make a comment, but she stayed silent without even looking at him.

'We stream our Sunday sermons on our YouTube channel for those who can't make it to church on the day. Something we started during the pandemic.' He looked down at his mother again, as if uncertain whether he should continue, but she didn't move. 'We had to mute the comments. People were posting threats like that letter, but we could never work out who they were or where they were coming from.'

'Did you ever report it?'

'No. Dad didn't want to make a fuss. He thought they were probably trolls from somewhere on the other side of the world.' He shook his head. 'Guess he got that wrong.'

They took their leave from the Holts and walked out to the car in silence. Pat was feeling a little uneasy. He knew people behaved in strange ways in the immediate aftermath of an unexpected death, but there was something about what he'd just witnessed that was beyond the reach of his intuition. He let it go as he opened the door and got into the car, knowing it would eventually rise into his conscious awareness if he didn't try to force it.

Lina started the car and reversed out of the driveway into the car park. Pat looked at their surroundings in the early morning light. The church property was on the edge of town. There were vineyards on its northern and western sides, a house surrounded by trees on its southern side, and a row of houses across Chalk Hill Road on the eastern side.

'What do you think?' said Pat, thinking they probably had little chance of confirming Thomas Holt's alibi.

'She was pretty calm for someone whose husband has just been murdered.'

'Think she could have done it?'

Lina turned on to Chalk Hill Road. 'Too early to say, Pat. I think we need to talk to her sister to see if she saw him when she picked her up last night.'

'She was quick to show us the evidence to back up her alibi. Made me think she was prepared for the question.'

'You thinking she might have killed him before she went out?'

'Would explain why she knew he was dead when she got home,' said Pat, recalling the words Mrs Holt had said to them when he'd asked her if she'd checked to see whether her husband was dead or not.

'Maybe she's a bored housewife that watches a lot of crime shows on TV.'

Pat looked out at the greenery of the vines that stretched into the distance. He was always amazed at how green the vines were at this time of year, when every other piece of vegetation had been burnt to a brown crisp by the summer sun and lack of rain.

'I didn't pick up on anything that sounded like a motive for either of them,' said Lina.

'I guess the son has something to gain from his death,' said Pat, 'but nothing that wouldn't have been coming to him at the end of the year when his father retired.'

'We'll need to check out that YouTube channel he mentioned to see if we can get a lead on where their abusive comments came from.'

'Watching a few of his sermons should give us an idea of

what sort of firebrand preacher we're dealing with, if nothing else.'

'What makes you think he would have been a firebrand preacher?'

'The pastors of these community churches are what my dad called far right fundamentalist crackpots, you know, the type that are happy to tell the rest of us how to live our lives according to their interpretation of the bible, which is usually based on a literal reading of selected passages.'

Lina glanced at him. 'That's a big generalisation, Pat. For all we know, Pastor Holt may have been one of those Jesus is all about love and forgiveness types.'

'Then how do you explain the letter we found in his study, and the comments his son told us about on their YouTube channel?'

'Hmmm, I see what you mean but, in case you've forgotten, Jesus ended up like our pastor, even with all his preaching on love and forgiveness.'

'You think we should be looking for some Roman soldier, then?'

'Might explain the arrow, Pat, but we'll need to find one that's converted to Islam, if that letter's genuine.'

'That's something else we need to get to the bottom of.'

CHAPTER 4

McLAREN VALE, the gateway to one of South Australia's most accessible wine regions, and often inundated with visitors intent on enjoying the offerings of the region's numerous eating houses and wineries, had lost its local police station several years prior to Alastair Holt's death, due to a lack of community demand for police services.

Consequently, the incident room for the investigation into Alastair Holt's murder was set up at the Christies Beach Police Station, a twenty-minute drive away. Pat didn't have a problem with the location. Christies Beach was only a thirty-minute drive from where he lived, and not that much further from Police Headquarters in the city, where he and Lina were based.

Uniformed officers from Christies Beach, including those that had attended the crime scene and taken statements from the Holts and every resident of Galaxy Court, had been assigned to assist Pat and Lina with their investigation.

Pat skimmed through the reports placed on his desk by the first responders, noting their contents confirmed what their authors had told Lina at the scene. No-one had admitted to seeing or hearing anything, let alone anything unusual.

'I've managed to get onto Georgina Saddler,' said Lina. 'She works at Noarlunga Library, which is just up Beach Road from here. She's expecting us.'

'Let's go and have a chat with her, then.'

When they arrived at the Noarlunga Library, Pat was mildly surprised by the aura of self-assurance projected by the woman who introduced herself as Georgina Saddler. He'd been half expecting a clone of the timid, soft-spoken widow of their victim they'd met earlier.

Georgina ushered them into one of the library's study rooms, where they took seats around a small table in the centre of a glass enclosed space usually occupied by students from the adjoining TAFE College.

'How can I help you, Sergeant?'

'I presume you're aware we're investigating the death of your brother-in-law, Alastair Holt?'

'Your colleague did mention it when she called.' Georgina smiled in Lina's direction.

'Have you spoken with your sister since you heard about her husband's death?' said Pat, wondering about the reliability of the answers he was about to get to his questions.

'Caught up with her before coming to work this morning,' said Georgina. 'Poor thing, she's been up all night. Said you'd interviewed her and Thomas.'

'Talking to family members is standard procedure in cases like this,' said Pat, opening his notebook. 'Now, we'd just like to confirm a few things your sister told us about last night.'

'Oh, what sort of things?'

'She told us she was out with you last night. Is that correct?'

Georgina crossed her arms over her chest and leant back in her chair. 'Yes. We were at Vasarelli's. We go there on the fourth Thursday of the month with Sarah and Rose for a girls' night out.'

'I understand you picked up your sister around seven-fifteen.'

Georgina nodded. 'That sounds about right.'

'Did you get out of your car at your sister's house?'

'No. I don't get out when I pick her up on a Thursday night. Alastair doesn't appreciate me coming in and taking up his precious time.' Georgina smiled and leant forward towards Pat, resting her elbows on the table between them. 'Thursday night is when, sorry, I'm not used to talking about him in the past. I mean, it was when he wrote his sermon for the following Sunday. He wanted us out of the place so he could concentrate.'

'Did you see him at all when your sister came out to the car?'

'He usually stands in the doorway and waves,' said Georgina, frowning and moving her eyes to her left. 'I'm pretty sure I saw him in the doorway last night.'

'Pretty sure or definite?' said Pat.

'Is that important?' said Georgina, frowning again before her face lit up with a smile. 'Oh, I see. You want to know if he was alive when Marianne left home. Is that it?'

'Yes,' said Pat.

'He waved,' said Georgina. 'He was wearing grey shorts and a light blue shirt.'

That tallied with the clothing Pat had seen on the body. 'What time was it when you dropped your sister home?'

'Just before eleven.'

'Did you see any sign of Alastair when you dropped her off?'

'No, but I noticed the light in his study was still on, which was unusual. He'd usually be in bed when I dropped Marianne home on a Thursday night. He was an early riser. Liked to be in bed no later than ten.' Georgina shrugged. 'At the time, I thought he must have been having a few problems sorting out his sermon but, as we know now, that wasn't the case, was it?'

'Unfortunately not,' said Pat. 'Did you stay long enough to see your sister open the front door?'

Georgina shook her head. 'I wish I had. It must have been terrible to open that door and see what she saw.'

'You weren't to know.'

'None of us were to know,' said Georgina. 'How could we?'

Pat gave her a few moments to collect her thoughts.

'So, just to confirm,' said Pat, when she had regained her composure, 'the last time you definitely saw him alive would have been around seven-fifteen when you picked your sister up?'

'Yes.'

'Will you sign a statement to that effect?'

'Yes, of course.' Georgina locked eyes with Pat. 'You'll have a time of death, won't you? Surely you don't think Marianne killed him when she got home, do you?'

'It's too early for me to have any ideas about who may

have killed him, Mrs Saddler, which is why we're here talking to you,' said Pat, giving her what he hoped was his disarming smile. 'We'll have a better idea of his time of death after the post-mortem but, for now, you've confirmed he was still alive at seven-fifteen.'

Georgina leant back in her chair.

'How well did you know, Alastair?' said Pat.

'Marianne's been married to him for thirty-five years, and he's been the pastor of our church for all that time as well, so I guess you could say I knew him pretty well.'

'Well enough to know if he had any enemies?'

'He was a good man, Sergeant. He devoted his life to God and helping others, but, as you probably already know, anyone who stands up for biblical values these days is not popular with everybody. I'm sure there are people out there who don't agree with what Alastair preached but, honestly, I have no idea who would've wanted to kill him.' Georgina looked at Pat. 'It's not something you think about living in a place like McLaren Vale.'

'I guess not,' said Pat. 'Thanks for agreeing to see us.'

'When do you want me to sign that statement?'

'DC Palumbo will call you when she has it ready for you to sign.'

They'd had an early start, so after interviewing Georgina Saddler, they headed into the city. Pat checked his messages while Lina drove. There was nothing that couldn't wait.

'What did you make of Georgina?' said Pat, slipping his phone back into his pocket.

'Seemed genuine enough.'

'Bit different to her sister.'

'You don't think the wife is genuine?'

Pat rubbed his chin. 'I'm not sure about the wife. Don't know what it is, but something's not quite right there. No, what I meant was, apart from their physical resemblance, I wouldn't have picked them as sisters.'

'Yeah, know what you mean, Pat. This one was full of life but, then again, her husband wasn't murdered last night.'

'I'm not sure Mrs Holt would have that much life in her even if her husband was still alive,' said Pat. 'The impression I'm getting is of someone defeated by life. Maybe that's what's worrying me about her.'

'You think we might be dealing with the fallout of an unhappy marriage?'

'She wouldn't be the first woman to knock off her husband,' said Pat, 'but she doesn't strike me as the type.'

'There's a type? I thought we were supposed to keep an open mind about that and follow the evidence.'

'Touché,' said Pat. 'You're right. We need to get our hands on some hard evidence and see where it leads us.'

'We should have the initial crime scene report by tomorrow. That should help.'

CHAPTER 5

AT THE END of her post-mortem examination of Alastair Holt's body, the pathologist advised Pat that his victim, a relatively healthy sixty-five-year-old male, had died as the result of a crossbow bolt penetrating his heart sometime between eight and eleven o'clock on the Thursday night his body had been found.

That puts Marianne Holt in the clear, as far as being the person who had fired the crossbow, thought Pat. 'Anything on the body that could identify who shot him?'

'There's nothing under the fingernails, if that's what you mean, Sergeant. I'll let you know what we find from the analysis of the fibres we've lifted from his clothing.'

'Okay.'

'Oh, and I've sent the crossbow bolt to Ballistics to see if they can tell us anything about it. Unfortunately, it's clean. Whoever handled it before firing it into your victim was wearing gloves.'

Somebody who knew what he was doing then, thought Pat. 'Thanks.'

As he made his way back to his desk in the incident

room, Pat ruminated on what he knew. His victim had been killed after opening the front door of his home to someone in the fading light of a summer evening. Would it have made any difference to his victim if he'd known the person at his door or not? Possibly not. He was a pastor, after all, and probably used to having people call on him at all hours. How much time would he have had to react once he'd spotted the crossbow? It wasn't as if a crossbow was an inconspicuous weapon like a knife or a handgun, was it?

Pat wondered if the assailant had stood on the threshold of his victim's doorway with his weapon at the ready and fired as soon as his target had opened the door, not giving his victim time to react. That would explain the position the body was found in. But the door had been closed and locked after he'd been killed, according to the victim's wife. That possibly meant the murderer had known how to lock it. At the very least, it meant the killer had to have touched the door or the door handle and closed the door, even if the locking had been fortuitous. And even if he'd been wearing gloves, what about footprints or drops of perspiration on the porch outside the door? Surely, he must have left some trace of his presence.

A crossbow isn't exactly silent, thought Pat. Firing one makes less noise than a gun but it generates an audible sound. According to his overnight internet research, the level of that sound depended on the size of the bow, the nature of its construction, and how well it was maintained. And, apparently, they made sounds when you were getting them ready to fire, especially those with metal parts.

Pat tried to picture their killer. He was obviously confident his target would open the door and that he could approach the house and depart without being seen or heard, which is precisely what the near neighbours had claimed. Whatever noise the crossbow had made, it had obviously not been loud enough to be heard above the sound of the TV programs the neighbours had been watching at the time. He supposed the killer could have used a silent mode of transport like a bike, or simply arrived and departed on foot, with his weapon hidden in a large sports bag, like the ones he saw kids walking around with on Saturday mornings.

Then there was the letter. Was it a clue or a red herring? Was its arrival on the day of the murder significant or pure coincidence? Was it for real or was it someone's idea of a prank designed to stir up the pastor in response to his preaching? That was something else he'd have to look into. What exactly had his victim been posting to YouTube for his followers and detractors to watch?

As he took his seat at his desk, Pat hoped the crime scene report would give them something to work on.

Lina looked up from her screen. 'This doesn't look promising, Sarge.'

'What do you mean?'

'They only picked up three sets of prints from the crime scene. The victim's, the wife's, and the son's. Either she's extremely thorough when it comes to housecleaning or nobody's visited them in ages.'

'Anything from the door or the porch?'

'Nothing that's not connected to the family.'

'Any sign the door handle was wiped down?'

'Clear prints on the door handle from all three family members,' said Lina. 'You'd expect the victim's would have been smudged or erased if someone had wiped down the door handle before the wife and son returned to the house.'

Pat put his hands behind his head and leant back in his chair, wondering if the killer had slipped a wire or something similar around the handle to pull the door shut. That would explain the lack of damage to the victim's prints on the handle, he supposed. 'Any luck with the letter?'

'It's got the victim's prints all over it, but no-one else's. Looks like the wife and son at least had the sense not to touch it.'

'And the envelope?'

'The wife's and the victim's, which would be right, seeing she told us she collected the mail and the victim obviously opened the envelope.'

Pat drummed his fingers on his desk, trying to make sense of what Lina was telling him. 'So, we're dealing with the invisible man. Nobody saw him and he didn't leave a trace.'

'Or it's them,' said Lina.

'We've got a pile of people saying she was in that restaurant until closing time, Lina, but the son doesn't have a watertight alibi, though, does he?'

'We'll need to show he wasn't at home when the murder happened,' said Lina. 'Did you get an update on the time of death?'

'Between eight and eleven pm,' said Pat, scratching his ear. 'Let's check the movements of his mobile for that night and have a chat with his neighbours.'

'What's happening with the crossbow bolt?'

'It's with Ballistics to see what they can make of it.'

'No fingerprints?'

'Clean as a whistle, apparently.'

'There aren't that many places you can legally buy a crossbow, you know, Sarge, and you have to provide proof of age and a legal reason for wanting it.'

'Which means they'd have a database of their customers,' said Pat.

'Of course, our killer could have made his own. I found a set of instructions on the net last night that even I could follow.'

'That bolt looked professionally made to me,' said Pat, 'but I guess Ballistics will work out if it isn't.'

'Want me to start chasing up the retailers?'

'Let's wait and see if we're dealing with a home-made item or not,' said Pat. 'I'd be surprised if someone who's as invisible as this guy appears to be left a record of purchase for us to find.'

'He wouldn't be the first criminal genius tripped up by his own paper trail.'

'I guess there could be a black market in crossbows,' said Pat, 'seeing as the government is about to ban hunting with bows and arrows.'

'At least Parks and Wildlife will have a list of people with hunting permits if we need to go down that rabbit hole.'

'Let's see where young Holt's mobile was on Thursday night,' said Pat, 'and then we'd better go for a drive and speak to his neighbours.'

CHAPTER 6

ON HER WAY TO start her Friday afternoon shift behind the service counter at Moana Pharmacy, Grace Williams was listening to the midday news on the car radio. She was paying scant attention to the national headline stories about the political scene in Canberra and the ongoing wars in faraway places. She'd heard it all before. But she nearly lost control of the vehicle when the newsreader started the local news with the story of the death, suspected homicide, of Pastor Alastair Holt.

With her heart thumping in her chest, Grace pulled over to the side of the road and burst into tears. Frantic, she searched the interior of the car until she located the box of tissues she knew was there somewhere. Slumping back into her seat once she had the box in her hand, she pulled out a handful of tissues, blew her nose and wiped at her eyes.

For the next few minutes, she sat staring ahead, seeing nothing, and breathing slowly until her sense of panic subsided. She blew her nose again, then looked at her face in the mirror on the back of the sun visor while she dabbed at her eyes with a tissue.

She took a few moments and touched up her makeup before resuming her drive to work. With the ever-increasing costs of living her income had to absorb, she couldn't afford not to show up, no matter how disturbing the news of Alastair's death was. The true nature of her relationship with Alastair was a secret that not even Sophie, their daughter, knew about.

If anyone asked, she decided she'd say she had just received some bad news about a friend dying. She hoped that would be close enough to the truth for her to get through her shift without giving herself away.

Grace's affair with Alastair had started in the months following her husband's death. She'd only been married for a couple of years before finding herself a young widow, when a work accident had claimed her John's life.

Pastor Holt had officiated at their wedding, so it was only natural that she had turned to him for consolation. At first, Alastair had been very understanding and supportive and had encouraged her to rebuild her life.

When her compensation payment had come through, he'd helped her sort out her finances so she could keep the apartment she and John had purchased a few streets back from the beach at Moana. But, by that time, she had become emotionally dependent on his support and, without realising how she'd been gently manipulated, was soon having sex with him every time he called to visit.

She couldn't help herself. She'd fallen in love with the Alastair she'd come to know, despite him being a married man twenty years her senior, and her pastor. The sex with

Alastair turned out to be so much more satisfying than any of the sex she'd experienced with John.

In those first few months of him visiting, she couldn't get enough of him, and she worried about his wife finding out about them. Alastair had reassured her there was nothing to worry about. He'd told her all about his meek and mild Marianne, who believed whatever he told her. Their sex might have been illicit, but it was wonderful, and she'd chosen to believe his every word despite her worries of being found out.

After their first year of secret meetings, she'd tried to break off the affair. To her way of thinking, it hadn't seemed right that the pastor of her church was having wild sex with her, sometimes several times a week, when he had a wife and was preaching about wives being faithful to their husbands. But Alastair wouldn't hear of it. He'd told her a string of things she knew were lies, but which she'd preferred to believe because it meant he wouldn't let her end their affair.

Then, they'd had a condom mishap, and she'd fallen pregnant with Sophie. She'd expected Alastair to discard her or at least demand an abortion. But he didn't do either, and that cemented their relationship, even though she understood she would always be the other woman, the one in the shadows, the lover he would never acknowledge.

She'd gone on having sex with him whenever he called around on his pastoral visits, especially on those mornings when Sophie was at school. They'd even spent the Wednesday morning before he'd been murdered entangled in her queen sized double bed, talking about his plans for his impending retirement.

Now, sitting in the staff kitchen, Grace didn't know what to do. She was definitely going to miss the child support money Alastair had been sending her since Sophie had been born. Losing that was going to make things difficult for her and Sophie. She'd have to see if she could increase her hours or think about finding a better-paying job.

She looked at her reflection in the mirror above the sink as she washed her coffee cup. Her face was holding up. As she went back into the shop to resume restocking shelves, a task that never seemed to end, she wondered whether she should stay in the shadows or make her relationship with Alastair known, or if she could persuade Marianne to pay her for keeping her mouth shut.

CHAPTER 7

MARIANNE REALISED she had a problem when the forensic cleaners presented her with their account for payment within seven days. The only access to money she had ever had was through a credit card attached to Alastair's account, and that card had a restrictive two thousand dollar limit, most of which she'd used for their grocery shopping in the month prior to his death.

'Thomas, how am I going to pay this?' She held out the account for him to read. 'I don't have any money.'

'Don't worry, Mum. We'll sort it out.'

'I don't even know how many accounts we have,' said Marianne, recalling Thursday night's conversation about coercive control and bank accounts. 'Your father always looked after the finances.'

'Don't you have a credit card?'

'Yes, but it's attached to Alastair's account. I don't have an account in my name.'

'Which bank is the account with?'

'The Commonwealth,' said Marianne, 'but I don't know if that's the only account he had.'

'It's okay, Mum. We'll sort it out,' said Thomas. 'Where did Dad keep his wallet? His cards will be in there.'

'In the top drawer of his bedside cabinet, unless he had it on him.'

'I'm pretty sure it wasn't on the list of items the police gave us. Do you want me to have a look?'

'No, I'll get it.'

Marianne went into the bedroom she'd shared with Alastair. Sticking out from under the bed, his black slippers caught her eye. She pushed them under the bed with her foot and walked to the bedside cabinet on what had been Alastair's side of the bed. She'd deal with his stuff when she was ready, and that wasn't today.

She pulled out the top drawer of the bedside cabinet and extracted Alastair's wallet from among the assortment of keys, watches, and pocket knives he'd kept in the drawer. She opened the wallet. It held a wad of notes, which she quickly ascertained amounted to eight hundred and fifty dollars, and two Mastercards. One, like the card in her purse, bore Commonwealth Bank branding. The National Australia Bank had issued the other. Both were in Alastair's name. Mystified, she wondered why he would have accounts with two banks. She couldn't recall him ever saying anything about having an account with the National Australia Bank. It made little sense to her.

She returned to the kitchen, where Thomas was busy making them each a cup of instant coffee.

'Look, he's got two credit cards.' She held them out for Thomas to see. 'I never knew he had an account with the National.'

'Find any cash?'

'Eight hundred and fifty dollars in fifty-dollar notes.'

'Better keep that for your immediate needs,' said Thomas, pouring their coffees. 'Let's go into the study and use the computer to find out what we need to deal with these banks.'

While Thomas scrolled through the information about deceased estates on the bank's website, Marianne decided to explore the contents of Alastair's three-drawer filing cabinet. It had stood silently on the floor next to his desk for years, but she'd never been invited to familiarise herself with its contents. In fact, afraid of how Alastair would respond if he'd found her snooping, she'd never dared to pry until now.

It didn't take her long to discover that the top two drawers were full of documents related to Alastair's role as pastor of Southern Vales and that he'd used the bottom drawer for his personal documents. Which was where she located a folder full of bank statements.

Marianne extracted the folder and sat in Alastair's reading chair with the folder open in her lap. She flipped through the statements and was surprised to see her name listed on the Commonwealth account as well as Alastair's.

'Look at this, Thomas. What does it mean?'

Thomas took the statement from his mother, spread it out on the desktop, and then ran his finger down through the entries. 'This looks like the account Dad's stipend was paid into.'

'It's got my name on it.'

'It's a joint account, which, according to this,' said Thomas, pointing to the screen on Alastair's laptop, 'means you should have access to the money in it.'

'How will I be able to do that?'

'We'll talk to the bank. Don't worry. They'll sort it out.'

'What about this account at the National Bank?' Marianne handed him the statement.

'Looks like an everyday transaction account with a debit card attached to it.' Thomas ran his finger down the page. 'There appears to be a regular monthly transaction. Here, look!' He pointed at the entries on the statement. 'There's a transfer of eight hundred dollars to the same account number every month.' He turned the page over. The first transaction listed on the second page was a five-thousand-dollar ATM cash deposit and the closing balance shown at the bottom of the page, after six more transfers, was in excess of fifteen thousand dollars. Thomas wondered where the money had come from.

'Who would he have been sending money to every month?' said Marianne.

'Can't tell from this, Mum. It's only got an account number. We'll have to see if they'll tell us whose account it is if you really want to know,' said Thomas, picking up the statement to hand back to her. 'There was over fifteen thousand dollars in this account, Mum. Any idea where Dad was getting thousands of dollars in cash from three years ago?'

Marianne shook her head. 'He never told me anything about where his money came from. I always assumed everything came from his stipend or the work he picked up during vintage.'

'Is there a more recent statement?'

Marianne rifled through the National Australia Bank statements. 'No.'

'Maybe he closed the account,' said Thomas, wondering what had happened to the rest of the money.

Marianne picked up the National Australia Bank branded Mastercard. 'The expiry date on this card is for March next year.'

'We'll have to follow up with them to see if it's still open,' said Thomas, turning back to the screen of the laptop. 'I'll just finish reading this so I'll know what we'll need to take when we go to the bank.'

Marianne turned her attention back to the bottom drawer of the filing cabinet. Alastair's will had to be in there somewhere. She was sure they'd need to find that document before going to the bank. At least she knew the will existed, and that she had been named as the beneficiary of his estate, in the event she survived him, and that Thomas had been named as the executor. That was one thing Alastair had not kept from her. In fact, much to her surprise at the time, he'd insisted on her being present when he'd had it drawn up.

With Marianne distracted by her search for Alastair's will, Thomas removed the small notebook in which his father had recorded his usernames and passwords from its hiding place between the bibles on the desktop and slipped it into his shirt pocket.

He wanted to discover his father's online secrets before someone else exposed them, but decided he'd do that research on his laptop when he got home. He couldn't see a reason for disturbing his mother's peace of mind if he didn't have to. To his way of thinking, she didn't need to know what Alastair had been up to any more than what she already did, unless it would have a direct impact on her.

He knew his father had treated his mother badly. He'd

been a witness to the contradictions between his father's preaching and his actual living out of the biblical values he was so proud of proclaiming. But he'd discovered a different understanding of those values during his preparation for the ministry he was taking on in his father's footsteps.

As he joined his mother at the kitchen table to review his father's will, Thomas hoped he'd be able to undo some of his father's excesses, especially now Alastair was no longer around to object to the style of preaching and living he preferred.

CHAPTER 8

PAT SCRUTINISED the location data of Thomas Holt's mobile phone for the night his father had been killed. The details revealed the phone had not moved between six-thirty and nine minutes after eleven on the night in question and identified its location as being in the vicinity of the Southern Vales Community Church building on Chalk Hill Road.

He turned his attention to the call log. The only incoming call in that time period had been the one Holt's mother had made shortly after eleven. Thomas had made no outgoing calls until he'd called triple zero at twenty-three minutes after eleven.

Pat looked across the desk he was sharing with Lina in the incident room at Christies Beach. 'This clearly shows his phone was where he says he was on the night his father was killed.'

'Doesn't prove he was there, though, does it?'

'Be pretty hard to show he wasn't there around eleven. That's when he answered the call from his mother, and the data shows his phone moved to her location before he called triple zero.'

'True, but where was he between eight and eleven? All we got from the neighbours was that his car was seen in the driveway around seven, and that there was a light on in his shed around ten.'

Pat thought they were probably clutching at straws, thinking of Thomas as a suspect. 'If we look at it from another angle, no-one's reported seeing him leave the property or being in the vicinity of his parent's house in Galaxy Court.'

'Yeah, but no-one said they actually saw him at home that night either, Pat. We've only got circumstantial evidence supporting his claim of being home alone.'

Pat scratched his head. He didn't like it when he couldn't determine whether an alibi was genuine or not. 'What'd be his motive? He was already in line to take over his father's job, and it's not as though getting it a few months earlier than planned would be much of a motive for murder.'

Lina gave him one of those smiles that made him think of Angela. 'Come on, Pat. Not all murders are about money. Perhaps there's more to this family set-up than meets the eye.'

'What, you think our dead pastor abused his own son, and this is payback?'

Lina shrugged. 'Honestly, I don't know, Pat, but it's not beyond the realm of possibilities, is it?'

'I know we wouldn't be doing our job if we weren't looking at the family, and it's not only the son we need to think about. There's something about the wife I can't put my finger on, but we need to follow the evidence and not get carried away speculating about what could have happened.'

'What about the letter? That's evidence, isn't it?'

Pat looked at his watch. 'About to find out. I've got a call booked with Counter-Terrorism in ten.'

———

'Your letter looks like a hoax, Pat. We've got no intel suggesting there's an active ISIS cell targeting anyone in South Australia, let alone the pastor of a small community church. Besides, ISIS groups use social media channels to get their message out. If they wanted to threaten your victim, it's more likely they'd have posted their threat as a comment on his YouTube channel or broadcast it on one of their own channels, and we've seen no sign of that.'

'His son said there had been some abusive comments on their YouTube channel.'

'We had a look at that, Pat. I'd say this guy had more problems with the LGBTQI community than with any Islamic group, and most of the abusive comments on his channel originate from overseas. There's only a couple of threatening comments from IP addresses in Australia, and they're not local either. Besides, if this was ISIS, they'd have claimed responsibility by now. They want the world to know when they strike. To be honest, I reckon this is someone's idea of a sick joke.'

Pat thanked his opposite number from Counter-Terrorism and ended the call. Then he sat and stared at the cloudless blue sky visible through the windows and ruminated.

If there were no terrorists behind the threat, he was left with LGBTQI activists, the local community, and the family, unless Holt's murder had been a random act by a crazed individual with a crossbow. The Southern Vales

Community Church had around two hundred members, made up of less than fifty families, and he wondered how many of them would be likely to have both a grudge against their pastor and a crossbow.

Not many, he thought, and decided it would probably be easier to find out who among them owned a crossbow than it would be to discover who held a grudge against their victim, unless that turned out to be public knowledge within the community.

His phone rang, interrupting his stream of thought.

'DS Travers.'

'Hi, Pat. Matt Burgess from Ballistics. I've been looking at your crossbow bolt.'

'Find anything I can hang a hat on, Matt? I need something to work with on this one.'

'You're looking for someone who makes his own bolts, Pat.'

'Would that be unusual for someone owning a crossbow?'

'It's not unheard of. There are archers that make their own arrows, but I'd say you were looking at a smaller subset with crossbow users. There aren't that many of them around these days. I'd suggest you focus on target shooters. They're more likely to be making their own bolts. I'll send you the write up.'

'Thanks, Matt.'

Pat put his phone back into his pocket and looked across the table at Lina. 'You'd better get onto compiling that list of crossbow owners. We need to find someone that makes his own bolts and likes to hand deliver threatening letters to his victims. Counter-Terrorism reckon there's no known active ISIS cell around here.'

'So, they're saying that letter is a distraction?'

'Might not even be connected with Holt's death,' said Pat. 'Counter-Terrorism think it's probably someone's idea of a joke.'

Lina shrugged. 'Bit of a coincidence it showing up the same day he was killed, though. Don't you think?'

Pat rubbed his chin. 'Maybe the joke's on us.'

CHAPTER 9

OVER THE NEXT TWO WEEKS, while Lina focused on tracking down and interviewing crossbow owners, and verifying their alibis for the night Alastair Holt was killed, Pat interviewed the adult members of the Southern Vales Community Church.

At the end of his round of interviews, Pat felt he was no closer to finding out who had fired the shot that had killed their pastor or why. Every member had spoken highly of Pastor Holt. No-one thought he had enemies within the community when asked or said anything that suggested impropriety associated with his behaviour. The overall impression he'd gained from speaking to the church's members was they regarded their pastor as someone who had lived out the biblical values he'd preached.

Someone, obviously, didn't agree with the community's assessment of their pastor, thought Pat, as he typed up the report on his interviews. He wondered if he'd been lied to by a community intent on protecting its public image or if Alastair Holt had had a life beyond the scope of his role as pastor, a secret life he'd kept hidden even from his wife.

Pat had watched a few of the sermons Holt had published on the church's YouTube channel. The man came across as a fundamentalist Christian who preached what Pat thought of as a right-wing conservative world view steeped in old-fashioned biblical values. Not the sort of message that resonated with the modern world, but one which seemed to be mainstream for the world Holt had lived in. Pat couldn't imagine anyone outside the church community watching its YouTube channel content, unless by accident. Even the comments that had concerned the Holts had come from viewers in faraway places, from people who'd probably only stumbled across the recordings thanks to Google's algorithms.

As Pat was ruminating, Lina returned to her spot across the table from him.

'Making any progress?' said Pat.

'I've hit a wall,' said Lina. 'Not one of them makes his own bolts, and I can't place any of them in McLaren Vale on the night of Holt's death.'

Pat drummed his fingers on the tabletop. 'So, we're looking for someone who's outside the system, someone who's made his own weapon and taken a dislike to our pastor.'

'Unless we're dealing with a totally random act of violence.'

'We're missing something, Lina,' said Pat, shaking his head. 'In my experience, people don't just rock up at your front door and shoot you for no reason. There's always a reason for murder, even if it's something trivial, and that reason will tell us who we're looking for. We just have to work out what it is.'

Pat heard the ding of an arriving email and glanced at his

screen, but it wasn't his inbox that had triggered the notification. He looked across the table at Lina, who was reading
something on her screen.

'This could be interesting, Pat. The NAB has just got
back to me with the details of who Holt was sending eight
hundred dollars to every month. The account it's being trans-
ferred to belongs to a Grace Williams, who lives in Moana,
and the transfer's been going on for years.'

'I think I interviewed a Grace Williams,' said Pat, flip-
ping through his notebook. 'Here it is. Works at the Moana
Pharmacy. Told me Holt had officiated at her wedding and
been very supportive after her husband was killed in a work
accident. Said he was a wonderful man who'd be missed, but
didn't mention anything about him sending her money,
though.'

'Bit sus, don't you think? Especially seeing the money is
coming from his personal finances and not from a church
account.'

'Perhaps we'd better go and have a chat with her.'

Lina parked in front of the Moana Pharmacy. Pat got out of
the car and went into the pharmacy and showed his ID to
the woman behind the counter.

'I'm looking for Grace Williams.'

'She won't be in until after she's picked up her daughter
from school. Do you want me to ask her to call you?'

Pat's ears pricked up. A daughter? Grace hadn't
mentioned a daughter when he'd interviewed her a week
ago. 'I have her home address,' said Pat. 'I'll drop around and
see if she's home. Thanks.'

Pat got back into the car. 'She's on the late shift today. Let's try her home address.'

'Want me to try her number?'

'Let's see if she's home first,' said Pat, writing in his note-book. 'Apparently, she has a daughter.'

'Thought you interviewed her?'

'She didn't say anything about having kids. I got the impression she hadn't remarried, so I didn't ask.'

Lina turned and looked at him. 'Do you think this money could be a child-maintenance payment?'

'Only one way to find out.'

Grace Williams' apartment was one of a group of three located a few streets back from the beach at Moana. Pat imagined Grace gazing out to sea from the balcony on the upper level as they parked in the street in front of her home.

There was a small red car parked in the driveway in front of the garage's open roller door. Although Pat assumed Grace was home, no-one answered the doorbell when he rang it. He waited for a couple of minutes and then called her mobile number. The call went through to voice mail.

'I can hear it ringing,' said Lina, peering in through the front window of the apartment. 'I can't see any movement.'

Pat slipped on a rubber glove and tried the door handle. The front door was locked. 'See if you can get around the back. I'll check the door in the garage.'

Pat heard the latch on the side gate click as Lina made her way around to the rear of the building. He looked over his shoulder. There was no-one about, not even a nosy neigh-bour twitching a curtain. He entered the garage. It was empty, except for a bicycle with a flat tyre propped up against the rear wall, which, given the dimensions of the space, didn't surprise Pat. It was barely big enough to park a medium-sized car and squeeze yourself out of the driver's side door before opening the door into the apartment.

Pat tried the door with his gloved hand. It wasn't locked. He cracked it open. 'Police!'

There was no response. He pushed the door fully open and stopped. Grace Williams lay sprawled on her back in a pool of blood, an open-eyed stare frozen on her face and a black object protruding from her chest. An object, Pat realised, he'd seen before, embedded in the chest of Alastair Holt.

While they waited for the scene of crime unit to arrive, Pat and Lina door-knocked the apartments of Grace's neighbours, including the doors of the houses opposite with a view of her apartment, without speaking to anyone. It looked like this section of Moana was a dormitory for people who worked elsewhere.

'We need to locate the daughter,' said Lina.

'We don't even know her name,' said Pat.

'Someone in the pharmacy where she works probably does,' said Lina. 'Give them a call.'

'Might be better if we do that in person.'

CHAPTER 10

PAT AND LINA entered Seaford Secondary College and approached the counter in front of a large wall sign in the school's colours welcoming them to the college.

'Can I help you?' said the woman at the counter.

'We need to speak to Sophie Williams,' said Pat, showing her his ID.

'Sophie's a minor,' said the woman. 'You're not allowed to interview her without her mother being present?'

'We're not here to interview her, I'm afraid,' said Pat. 'There's been an incident involving her mother.'

'Oh,' said the woman. 'I'll let the Principal know you're here. You can sort out the legalities with him.'

A few moments later they were sitting in the Principal's office with a balding middle-aged man, who'd introduced himself as Malcolm Weeks.

'This doesn't sound good, Sergeant.'

'I'm afraid it's not, Mr Weeks. Sophie's mother was found dead this morning.'

Mr Weeks swallowed. 'And you want me to tell her, is that it?'

'No, I want you to bring her here so we can tell her, but it would help if there was a counsellor or other support person with her when we do.'

'Oh, of course. I'll see if Jenny Evans is available. She's the Student Counsellor.'

They waited while Mr Weeks arranged for the Student Counsellor to collect Sophie from her class and bring her to his office.

'Do you have any next of kin details on record for Sophie?' said Pat.

'We should have an emergency contact number,' said Mr Weeks. 'That's often another family member. Let me see.' He turned to the computer on his desk and spent a few moments tapping on its keyboard. 'We've got a mobile phone number for Sophie's grandmother. She lives in Noarlunga. I'll print out the record for you.'

'Thanks,' said Pat.

As Mr Weeks handed the page from his desktop printer to Pat, there was a knock at the door. When Pat looked up, there was a girl with short blond hair, dressed in the school's summer uniform, standing in the doorway in front of a young woman with long dark hair dressed in a lightweight business suit.

'You wanted to see me, Mr Weeks?'

'Come in, Sophie, and shut the door,' said Mr Weeks. 'These people are from the police.'

A look of apprehension crossed Sophie's face as the Counsellor closed the door and directed her to a chair at the table where Pat and Lina sat. Pat wondered what mischief she'd been up to in her free time she thought she'd been caught out in.

'I'm Detective Sergeant Travers and this is Detective

Constable Palumbo. I'm afraid we have some upsetting news for you, Sophie.'

Sophie's eyes darted from Pat to Lina, and around to the Counsellor sitting beside her, before she faced Pat again. 'What do you mean?'

'I'm sorry, Sophie, but we're here to tell you your mother was found dead at home this morning.'

'How can she be dead? She drove me to school this morning.'

'I wish it wasn't true,' said Pat, 'but I'm afraid it is.'

Sophie burst into tears and collapsed into the Counsellor's waiting arms.

Pat didn't know what to say to comfort a fifteen-year-old girl in distress, so he waited until her sobbing subsided. When Sophie sat back up in her chair, he touched Lina's foot with his shoe under the table.

'This is not going to be easy, Sophie, but we're going to have to ask you some questions about your mum,' said Lina. 'We can't do that without an appropriate adult present, and now's probably not a good time. I know I wouldn't be able to think straight after what we've just told you.' Lina smiled at Sophie. 'You can have your grandmother with you when we interview you, or or another adult you trust, like someone here at school. Who would you like to be present?'

'Grandma,' said Sophie, wiping at her eyes with the back of her hand before taking the tissues offered by the Counsellor.

'We'll arrange for your grandmother to come and pick you up from school. Okay? Then we'll sort out a time with her for your interview. For now, we'll leave you with Ms Evans while we make contact with your grandmother. Okay?'

'Can't someone just take me home?'

Lina shook her head. 'I'm sorry, Sophie, but you won't be able to go home for a few days. Your house is a crime scene.'

Sophie's eyes opened wide. 'You mean someone's murdered my mother, and that's why she's dead?'

'Afraid, so,' said Pat, 'but we can't go into any of the details because we don't know what happened yet.'

'But you'll find out, won't you?'

'That's our job,' said Lina.

CHAPTER 11

PAT SAT at his computer in the incident room reading the crime scene report for Grace Williams' murder. There were no signs of a forced entry, meaning the victim had either let her killer in, or her killer had entered through the unlocked door from the garage.

Recalling that the roller door to the garage had been up when they'd arrived at the apartment, Pat scanned through the list of items found in the victim's car until he spotted a listing for a roller door remote.

He imagined Grace opening the roller door with the remote and entering her apartment through the garage after returning from dropping her daughter at school. He wondered why she hadn't driven into the garage, and why she hadn't locked the door behind her. Perhaps, he surmised, she'd planned to go out again and her killer had intercepted her while she was retrieving something from the apartment. That would explain the position of the body on the floor of the hallway immediately inside the door from the garage.

Strikingly similar to the execution of Alastair Holt, thought Pat. In both cases, it looked as if the killer had stood outside a door opened to him, fired a crossbow bolt into his victim's heart, and then disappeared without anyone seeing him. The killer was definitely a him in Pat's mind, even though he'd counselled Lina to keep an open mind on the subject of the killer's identity.

Pat leant back into his chair and looked at the images that formed part of the report. The bolt looked almost identical to the one they'd extracted from Holt's body. He wondered how long it would take Ballistics to confirm his assessment of the bolts being made by the same hands.

They hadn't released the specific details of how Holt had been killed, and here he was looking at an identical killing. He wondered what the likelihood of two people belonging to the same church community being killed in exactly the same way by two different killers would be. Not high, he concluded. It had to be the same perpetrator as far as Pat could see, which made him think there had to be a connection between the victims.

The crime scene investigators had dusted the apartment for prints and swabbed it for DNA. Pat noted that most of the prints and DNA samples collected matched those of Grace and Sophie Williams, which wasn't surprising, but a number didn't. Some were unidentified, meaning Forensics couldn't match them with anyone known to them, which wasn't all that unusual. What caught Pat's attention, however, was the finding that several of the foreign samples matched the fingerprints and DNA they had on record for Alastair Holt. The number of matches suggested Holt had been a frequent visitor to Grace's apartment, and not just to her living room. Pat wondered if he'd found the connection he was looking for. But before he could alert Lina to his discovery, his phone rang.

'DS Travers.'

'Sergeant, I've got a Mrs Stein at reception. She wants to talk to you about the Williams' case.'

That name rang a bell. Pat was pretty sure he'd interviewed someone by that name as part of his background checks on Alastair Holt. 'Put her in an interview room. I'll be right down.' He put his phone back into his pocket.

'What's up?' said Lina.

'There's a Mrs Stein at reception that wants to talk to us about Grace Williams.'

'Isn't she one of the people you interviewed?'

'Maybe she wants to tell us why Alastair Holts' fingerprints and DNA are all over Williams' apartment.'

'Are they?'

'Apparently they're in every room, including her bedroom.'

Pat opened the door to the interview room. The slim, grey-haired woman sitting at the table stood as they entered. He recognised her as one of the women he'd interviewed about Alastair Holt.

'Hello, Mrs Stein. This is my colleague, Detective Constable Palumbo. Please, sit down. You wanted to tell us something about Grace Williams?'

Pat and Lina sat at the table and waited.

Mrs Stein resumed her seat with a sheepish look on her face. 'First, I'd like to apologise for not being completely honest with you when you came to see me.'

'Oh, in what way?' said Pat.

Mrs Stein looked down at her hands resting in her lap. 'I

didn't want to speak ill of the dead or attract the attention of the church elders, so I didn't tell you a few things about Alastair that I now think you need to know.'

Pat's ears pricked up. The last time they'd spoken, she'd only referred to Alastair as Pastor Holt. 'What's made you change your mind?'

'I'm scared I might be next.'

Pat exchanged a glance with Lina, wondering why Mrs Stein thought she was in danger.

'Sounds like you want to make a statement. You okay if we record this? That'll make it easier for you to confirm our record of interview.'

'Do I need a lawyer to make a statement?'

'That depends, Mrs Stein. Are you volunteering information to help with our investigation or are you confessing to a crime?'

'I haven't done anything wrong, apart from not telling you everything I know about Alastair.' Mrs Stein looked at Pat. 'Am I in trouble?'

'That might depend on what you tell us,' said Pat. 'Why don't you start? If it sounds like you're confessing to a crime, we'll stop the tape and you can call your lawyer.'

Mrs Stein nodded. 'Sounds like a plan.'

Pat looked at Lina, who activated the video camera and went through the required preliminaries.

'Okay, Mrs Stein. What is it you want to tell us?'

'Everybody has probably told you how wonderful Alastair was, and it's true, he was a wonderful pastor. But there was another side to him that only Grace and I knew about. You see, we were his lovers.' She looked straight at Pat. 'There. I've said it.'

Finally, thought Pat. After hearing the same story about

their wonderful pastor from so many people, he'd started questioning its authenticity. Now, the pastor's image had a flaw in it. A crack he hoped would let him get behind the picture-perfect image the community obviously wanted to preserve of their beloved pastor.

'Is that why you think you're in danger?'

Mrs Stein nodded. 'You probably know by now that Grace's husband was killed in a work accident twenty years ago.' She paused and looked at Pat, as if expecting a response from him.

'We're aware of that,' said Pat

'She never remarried, but she has a fifteen-year-old daughter, Sophie. No-one's ever said a word about who that child's father is.' She paused and raised her eyebrows. 'I don't know what Grace told her parents, but Alastair was who she turned to for emotional support after her husband's death.' She smiled. 'I only found out about them when he started having sex with me when I did the same after my husband died. We never had children. I couldn't conceive, which was a bonus for Alastair.' She paused.

Pat waited, not wanting to interrupt her story.

'If anyone ever asked why he was visiting so often, all I had to say was it was part of his pastoral care program for widows and orphans.' She laughed. 'It was amazing. Nobody ever imagined what he was up to on those visits, but I knew he was visiting Grace as well. It didn't take much imagination to figure out he was giving her the same level of support he was giving me. In the end, Grace and I confided in each other.' She shrugged.

'I don't know if there were any others, but now that Grace and Alastair are both dead, I'm thinking somebody's found out about what Alastair was doing and wants to make sure there's nobody around to talk about it.'

One affair would be difficult enough to hide, thought Pat, especially in a small community, but it seemed Alastair Holt had kept two under wraps for years. Pat, in awe of the sheer arrogance of the man, wondered how it had all come undone. He felt Lina nudge him under the table and came back into the room. Mrs Stein was waiting for him to say something.

'It's possible they only found out about Alastair and Grace. Has anybody threatened you?'

'No-one's said anything to me,' said Mrs Stein, 'but they waited two weeks before going after Grace, didn't they? And, no-one threatened her as far as I know. She would have told me.'

'Sounds like you're assuming the same person killed them,' said Pat.

'I don't believe in coincidences, Sergeant. Someone knows, and they're cleaning up to protect the church's reputation.'

'Who do you think that might be?'

'I'd start with the elders. They've got the most to lose if the truth about Alastair gets out.'

'What about his family?'

'I think they already knew he wasn't the saint he made out to be. To be honest, I was surprised Thomas followed his father into the ministry, but after his last couple of sermons, I think I understand why now.'

'Oh?' said Pat.

'He's trying to wind back some of the more extreme views preached by his father. I hope he succeeds. God knows we need to become a more loving community if we're going to survive.'

Another crack in the community's facade, thought Pat, wondering what else would emerge over the course of their investigation. He hadn't thought of Thomas preaching a different message to that of his father. He felt Lina nudge his leg again.

'Well, you've certainly given us something to think about, Mrs Stein, and I can understand your concern for your welfare. Do you want us to arrange protection for you?'

Mrs Stein shook her head. 'When I leave here, I'm heading to the airport. I'm going to stay with my sister in Melbourne until you catch the bastard that killed my friends.'

'Will you be safe there?'

'Nobody here knows about my sister, Sergeant. She's a Catholic nun.'

Pat's mobile rang in his pocket as they were making their way back to the incident room.

'DS Travers.'

'Sergeant. Kathy Rice. Have you read my report yet?'

'I've had a look,' said Pat.

'There was something in the DNA results that piqued my interest, so I had some further analysis done. The results have just come back, and I thought you'd like to know straight away.'

Pat was intrigued. He didn't think he'd read anything about having further tests run on any of the samples in her report. Perhaps he'd missed it. 'What have you got for me?'

'Alastair Holt and Grace Williams are Sophie Williams' parents.'

'Are you sure?'

'As sure as I can be,' said Kathy. 'I'll send you an update to my report as soon as I've written it.'

'Thanks,' said Pat, ending the call and slipping his phone back into his pocket.

'Who was that?' said Lina.

'Kathy Price. She's just confirmed that Alastair Holt was Sophie Williams' father.'

Lina stopped walking. 'Do you think his wife knew?'

'Only one way to find out, but before we do that, let's see if there's been any contact between the Holts and Grace Williams since Alastair was killed.'

CHAPTER 12

LINA PARKED in front of the Holt residence in Galaxy Court, where a white VW Golf stood in the driveway.

'Looks like Thomas might be here,' said Pat.

'Two for the price of one,' said Lina, opening her door and getting out of the car.

Pat opened the gate in the front fence. It squeaked and made a loud click when he closed it behind them.

'No way you could sneak into this place through that gate,' said Lina.

'But you could probably jump over it if you wanted to sneak in,' said Pat. 'It's not that high.'

'I'd ask you to demonstrate, but I don't want to be explaining to Angela how you ripped your nice new suit pants.'

'Weren't you listening? I didn't say I could jump over it.' Pat grinned. 'Come on, let's see who's home.' He pressed the doorbell button, and they waited for someone to answer the ding dong sound they heard it make.

Pat was about to press the button again when the door

opened. 'Oh, hello,' said Thomas. 'Are you looking for me or Mum?'

'Is your mother home?' said Pat.

'Yes, she's out the back.'

'In that case, it would be convenient if we could talk to both of you.'

'Okay.'

Thomas led them through the house to the alfresco dining area that opened onto the garden in the backyard, where Marianne Holt sat at a wooden outdoor table in front of two coffee mugs and a plate of cupcakes.

Pat almost didn't recognise Marianne when she smiled at him in recognition. Her smile held so much energy it reminded him of her sister.

'Any news, Sergeant?'

'Do you mind if we sit?' said Pat, pulling out a chair.

'Of course not. Would you like a cup of coffee or something to eat?'

'No, we're right.' Pat waited for Thomas and Lina to sit at the table. 'We need to discuss a few things concerning Grace Williams.'

'She was a long-time member of our community,' said Marianne. 'Alastair officiated at their wedding. Poor girl. Her husband was killed at work not long after they were married. I can't believe she's dead.'

'Did Alastair have much to do with her, apart from seeing her when she came to church services?'

'She came to Alastair when her husband, John, yes, I think that was his name. Anyway, when he died, Grace was devastated. She would have only been in her mid-twenties. Alastair was good with people like that. He took God's directive to look after widows and orphans seriously.'

'What about more recently, say in the last year or so?'

'Alastair was always visiting people. Pastoral care, he called it. If there are records of his visits, they'll be in his diaries.' Marianne looked at Thomas. 'Have you had a look at them yet?'

'Not yet,' said Thomas, 'but I could get them and have a look if you like?'

'Perhaps before we go,' said Pat. 'Did he talk about his pastoral care visits?'

'Not really,' said Marianne. 'At least, not with me.'

'We talked about the general principles,' said Thomas, 'and I had started visiting people with him as part of my preparation for taking over as pastor, but I don't recall Grace being one of the people we visited.'

Pat glanced at Lina and folded his arms before resting them on the edge of the table.

'Grace has a fifteen-year-old daughter, Sophie,' said Lina. 'Do either of you know who her father is?'

The Holts exchanged a glance that did not escape Pat's attention.

'We were just talking about that before you arrived,' said Marianne. 'I'd always assumed Grace had a one-night stand or a short-term relationship that didn't work out. She never ever said who Sophie's father was, but Thomas was just telling me he thinks he might know.'

'Care to elaborate, Thomas?' said Lina.

'I found something in Dad's bank statements. He'd been paying hundreds of dollars a month to Grace for years.'

'Yes, we know,' said Pat, 'and we were wondering why he'd done that too.'

Thomas folded his arms and leant back in his seat. 'Initially, I thought Dad must have been supporting her out of charity, but she called me a couple of days before she was murdered. She wanted to know if Dad had left anything to Sophie in his will.' Thomas took a deep breath. 'I certainly wasn't expecting that, so I asked her why she thought he would.' He exhaled slowly and let his arms drop into his lap. 'That's when she told me Sophie was his daughter.'

'Did you believe her?'

Thomas shook his head. 'I didn't know what to believe. It's not like Dad ever told us he had a daughter. Anyway, I told her there were ways of finding out if what she was telling me was true or not.'

'How did she react to that?'

'She said she'd talk with her lawyer and get back to me, but I guess she didn't get the opportunity, given what's happened.'

'And did your father leave anything to Sophie?'

'No. The only people named in his will are me and Mum.'

'Forensics have run a few tests on the DNA found in Grace's apartment. They recovered a lot of Alastair's DNA from several rooms,' said Pat, 'and some of those tests confirm what Grace told you.'

They sat in silence as the Holts digested Pat's revelation.

Marianne looked up. 'What does that mean, legally? Will I have to look after her?'

'She's in the care of her grandparents,' said Pat, 'but they may lodge a claim against Alastair's estate for child maintenance when they find out. You might want to speak to a lawyer.'

'This will come out in the press, won't it?' said Thomas. 'That's going to be a PR disaster.'

'It will come out, eventually,' said Pat. 'Truth has a habit of doing that.'

They sat in silence for several moments.

'When were you going to tell us?' said Lina.

'Tell you what?' said Thomas.

'That Grace had told you that your father was Sophie's father.'

'I wanted to tell Mum first.'

'It's been nearly a week since Grace was killed,' said Lina.

'Took me that long to pluck up the courage to tell Mum.'

'Scared of your mother or is there something else you need to tell us?' said Pat.

'No, it's just that I think she's suffered enough, and this is going to be another embarrassment for her to live with.'

'What do you mean?' said Lina.

Thomas leant forward and rested his folded arms on the tabletop. 'Dad may have been a wonderful pastor and a great preacher, but he wasn't always easy to live with. In fact, he was a bit of a control freak with Mum and me when I was growing up. Mum never really had a life of her own. She had to be the pastor's wife, and Dad had some pretty firm ideas on what that meant.'

'It's alright, Thomas,' said Marianne. 'We don't have to protect his reputation anymore. Sounds like he's done a good job of destroying it all on his own. He was a difficult man to live with, Sergeant, unless I did what he wanted, and that wasn't always easy. But, I found a way. I'm not complaining. He's left me in a good position, financially speaking, and I can always sell up and move away if things get ugly here when the truth comes out.'

'Did either of you know about Alastair's relationship

with Grace before Thomas found those bank statements?' said Pat.

'I had no idea,' said Marianne.

'What about you, Thomas?'

'I knew nothing about it.'

'And did you do anything about it when you found out?'

'What do you mean?'

'Did you tell anyone, say one of the church elders?'

'No, not yet.'

'Take any action against Grace?'

Thomas sat up straight in his chair. 'Don't be ridiculous. Why would I do anything to Grace?'

'I'll take that as a no for now,' said Pat.

'I know you're just doing your job, Sergeant, but that's still an offensive question.'

'No offence intended, Thomas. Did you tell anyone else?'

'No. It's not something I wanted to spread around, but I can see now I'm going to have to tell the elders before it comes out in the media.'

'Just for the record, where were you both last Wednesday morning between the hours of nine and noon? said Pat. 'Mrs Holt?'

'I was here.'

'Anyone with you?'

'Rose, Rose Treloar. She dropped in for coffee just before ten and then we went to the city. Didn't get back until around four-thirty.'

'Thomas?'

'I was in my workshop making kites for the youth group. We're going kite flying this weekend.'

'Anyone with you?'

'No.'

'Were you there the whole morning?'

'Except for when I ducked into town for a coffee, around ten-thirty.'

'Where'd you go for coffee?'

'Kicco Espresso.'

Pat stood. 'Perhaps you can give me your father's diaries for the last couple of years on the way out.'

'Let's go around to Kicco Espresso,' said Pat, looking at his phone. 'It's in the shopping centre on the main street.'

'I could use a coffee,' said Lina.

'And we can confirm Thomas' alibi while we're there,' said Pat.

'Don't you believe his story, then?'

Pat shook his head. 'He might be a pastor, but as we've just heard, pastors don't always tell the truth.'

'Where is the world going to when you can't trust a pastor?' said Lina, as she eased the car away from the kerb.

'To hell in a handcart,' said Pat. 'At least, that's what my dad always used to say.'

Lina executed a three-point turn and headed towards McLaren Vale's central business hub. 'Have you watched any of Alastair's sermons?'

'One or two. Fundamentalism's not really my thing.'

'I don't get it,' said Lina. 'How can someone preach like that and then do the exact opposite and get away with it? I mean, why didn't Grace and that Stein woman expose him for being such a hypocrite?'

'Guess they were getting something out of it.'

'They would have had a hold over him, I suppose,' said Lina. 'It's not like he could have walked away from either of them without worrying about what they could do to his reputation by speaking out.'

'Can't see they'd have a motive for killing him though,' said Pat. 'Unless there was something else going on.'

'That's going nowhere, Pat. After all, Grace is dead too. It's got to be someone who didn't want the truth to come out or someone who wanted Alastair to be dead when it did. Here we are.' Lina turned into the shopping centre car park.

'What about the Holts? Do you think they could be behind these killings?'

'Interesting about Alastair being a control freak,' said Lina. 'I can see a motive there for Thomas. He sounds pretty protective of his mother. I could understand why he'd snap and kill an abusive father, but why would he kill Grace? He had the bank statements, so he'd have known we'd find out about the payments, and he seems to have some idea about DNA based paternity tests. It wouldn't have taken him much to realise we'd figure out who Sophie's father was after we'd asked him and his mother for DNA samples. '

'Unless he acted on impulse and didn't think things through,' said Pat. 'Come on, let's get some coffee and check his alibi.'

They got out of the car and started walking towards the coffee shop.

'Do you reckon she did it?'

Pat shook his head. 'She's got an alibi for the time of Alastair's death, and we've searched her house. No sign of a crossbow.'

'Perhaps we should search his house,' said Lina. 'Who

knows what else he's been making in that workshop of his, apart from kites and toys?'

'That might have to be an informal visit,' said Pat, 'unless we can uncover something that links him to one of the murders.'

'He didn't seem too concerned about the damage this will do to his father's reputation,' said Lina. 'Sounded like he was more concerned about how the news was going to impact his mother.'

'I thought she took it pretty well, considering,' said Pat, opening the door for Lina. 'She seemed like a different person today.'

'You're not wrong there. I thought she was more alive than the last time we saw her. Guess time does heal like they say.'

'Yeah,' said Pat, 'but not usually that quick.'

A few of the tables were occupied by people chatting over coffee and cake. Pat ordered their coffees and, after showing her his ID, asked if the woman serving knew Thomas Holt.

'He's a regular. Often drops in for a mid-morning coffee and a chat. Nothing like his father. That boy will talk to anybody, and he's a good listener, too.'

'Was he here last Wednesday morning around ten-thirty?'

She pointed to the small model kite hanging from the noticeboard on the wall just inside the door. 'That's when he bought that in to advertise his kite flying activity. The kids love him.'

CHAPTER 13

THOMAS TOOK a deep breath and exhaled slowly. Then he opened the door to the meeting room at the back of the church. He didn't particularly like being the bearer of bad news, and what he was about to tell the four men waiting for him, who had entrusted their spiritual life to his father's guidance, was definitely bad news.

The soft buzz of conversation stopped as soon as he opened the door. The sudden silence whenever he joined the elders for a meeting always left him thinking they were discussing things they didn't want him to know about, and today didn't feel any different even though he was the one with the secret.

'So, young Thomas, what's so important that it couldn't wait until next week's council meeting?' said Reg Hartwood, chairman of the Council of Elders and owner of the vineyard that bordered the northern and western boundaries of the church property.

Thomas acknowledged Sam Westwood, a winemaker for a local winery, Michael Knolls, who owned the local hardware store where he often shopped for his craft supplies, and

Henry Yates, the local building contractor who oversaw the maintenance of the church property.

'Thanks for agreeing to meet at such short notice,' said Thomas, taking his usual seat next to Henry. 'I had a meeting with the police earlier today.'

'Have they worked out who killed Alastair?' said Reg.

'No, they wanted to talk about Grace Williams.'

'What's that got to do with us?' said Reg.

'Calm down, Reg,' said Michael. 'Give the boy a chance to get it out.'

'You know Grace has a daughter, don't you?'

'Yes,' said Reg. 'There was a bit of a to-do when she was born. We only let Grace stay because your father persuaded us not to kick her out of the community. We all make mistakes, he said, and sometimes it's better to forgive than punish. At least, that's what I remember Alastair saying.'

'What's the relevance?' said Michael. 'We all know Sophie. We've watched her grow up.'

'I had a call from Grace a couple of days before she was murdered,' said Thomas. 'She claimed Dad was Sophie's father.'

'Did she offer you any proof?' said Reg.

'No, we talked about paternity testing, but she was killed before we could arrange anything,' said Thomas. 'Thing is, though, the police have told us their forensic testing confirms she was telling me the truth. Dad's Sophie's father.'

'How?' said Henry. 'How did they come to that conclusion?'

'DNA,' said Thomas. 'Apparently, there was a lot of Dad's DNA in Grace's apartment and they worked it out while they were trying to identify who had been there when she was killed.'

'Who else knows about this?' said Reg.

'Mum,' said Thomas, 'and the police were going to speak to Grace's parents after they left us.'

'How did Marianne take the news?' said Michael.

'She was devastated,' said Thomas, 'but she says there's no point denying it.'

'And Alastair's not here to face the music, is he?' said Reg. 'He's left that to us.'

'This could destroy the community when it comes out,' said Sam. 'We need to decide how we're going to handle this. This is going to be hard on you, Thomas.'

'Does anyone know if Alastair got her pregnant and then broke it off or was it an ongoing relationship?' said Reg.

'The police seem to think it was an ongoing relationship,' said Thomas. 'They told us they'd found Dad's DNA in every room of Grace's apartment.'

'What was he thinking?' said Sam. 'I thought he was happily married to Marianne.'

'That was the impression they always gave,' said Thomas, 'but no marriage is perfect.'

'I wonder if there were any others,' said Sam.

'When did Grace's husband die?' said Michael.

'Be at least twenty years ago,' said Henry.

'If he managed to keep their relationship a secret for as long as that, who knows how many other secrets he kept from us?' said Reg. 'We trusted him. We followed his guidance, listened to his preaching. Paid him to be our shepherd.'

'Community is going to expect us to step down,' said Michael. 'They'll see this as a colossal failure of governance.'

'You might not survive this either, Thomas,' said Reg. 'We appointed you on your father's recommendation.'

'I'll just have to trust God on that,' said Thomas.

'Could be an opportunity for community renewal,' said Sam. 'People have been saying they like what they hear when Thomas preaches.'

'Not sure I want to step aside,' said Reg. 'I've invested over thirty years in building up this community.'

'We should at least offer to resign and leave it up to the others to decide how we go forward,' said Henry. 'I think that would be the right thing to do.'

'We should pray about it before we make any final decisions,' said Reg. 'Can you lead us in prayer, Thomas?'

CHAPTER 14

PAT'S MOBILE rang as he was making his way to the incident room from the car park. 'DS Travers.'

'Oh, hello, Sergeant Travers. My name is Heather Fountain. I found your card in my letterbox. I hope this is a good time to call.'

This had to be someone living near one of their crime scenes, thought Pat. Someone who hadn't been home when he or Lina had knocked on their door to ask questions. 'Now's fine,' said Pat. 'How can I help you?'

'I live next door to Grace Williams. I've been away in Tasmania for the last two weeks and didn't know about Grace until I got home last night.' She stopped talking.

Pat heard her draw in a breath and waited while she regained her composure.

'I'm the only one around here that's home during the day, Sergeant. I might be able to help you identify who was visiting Grace before she was killed.'

'Are you home now?' said Pat.

'Yes.'

'What's your address?'

'I'm in number two, right next door to Grace.'

'I'm on my way.'

The door to number two was opened by a neatly dressed woman with grey hair and a wrinkle free face beneath a layer of immaculate make-up.

'Heather Fountain?' said Pat.

'Yes.'

'Detective Sergeant Travers,' said Pat, showing her his ID. 'This is Detective Constable Palumbo.'

'Please, come in,' said Heather. 'We can sit in here.' She pointed through an open doorway into her lounge room and closed the door behind them.

The decor reminded Pat of the lounge room in his parents' house before his mother had moved into a nursing home after his father's death. Trinkets of dubious value filled every nook and cranny. An untidy pile of books topped with a smartphone stood next to a recliner armchair. A television set surrounded by framed photographs stood in the corner opposite the doorway. A two-seater couch covered with an assortment of cushions took up most of the remaining space.

Heather sat in the recliner. 'I spend half my day sitting in here. Please, make yourselves comfortable.'

Pat sat next to Lina on the couch, noting the unobstructed view of the street frontage. Immediately, he understood why Heather had told them she spent half her day in the room.

'How long have you been living here?'

'About five years. I moved here a couple of years after my

husband died. We had a nice house in Woodcroft. Too big for one person.'

'How well did you know Grace?'

'She was very friendly,' said Heather. 'I looked after Sophie for her when she needed a sitter.'

'So, she trusted you?'

'I'm a retired schoolteacher,' said Heather. 'If I must say so myself, I've always been good with children.'

'What can you tell us about the people in Grace's life?' said Pat.

Heather smiled. 'When I first moved here, I thought Grace was having an affair with that Pastor Holt that was killed before I went to Tasmania. He visited her every Wednesday morning. Sometimes, he'd be there for twenty minutes, you know, enough time for a chat over a cup of coffee. Other times, he'd be there for a couple of hours. Enough time to do who knows what. Anyway, Grace always insisted he was only visiting in his role as her pastor. She even tried to get me to join their church.'

'And, did you?'

'I went to a couple of Sunday services.' Heather smiled. 'Not my scene, I'm afraid.'

Not mine, either, thought Pat, thinking of what he'd watched on the church's YouTube channel. 'Was she visited by anybody else?'

'That's why I called you, Sergeant. Grace had started seeing this other fellow a few months back. Sophie didn't like him. Said he gave her the creeps. Maybe that's why Grace broke it off a few weeks before I went to Tasmania.'

Pat wondered why Sophie hadn't mentioned anything about her mother seeing someone. 'Do you know this man's name?'

'Sophie said his name was Phil. He works for a company called Snowdon Electrical. I have a photo of his van.'

'Oh?' said Pat, wondering why she had taken the photo.

'I like to keep an eye on things,' said Heather. 'Helps to pass the time when I'm sitting here. You can't read all day.'

'When did you take this photograph?' said Pat, giving silent thanks for Heather being the type of nosy neighbour he liked to hear from.

'A month or so ago,' said Heather. 'I noticed his van was in our street nearly every time I went out for my morning walk. I thought he might be stalking her, especially after Sophie told me Grace had broken it off.'

'Did you tell Grace?'

'She said it was probably only a coincidence. He's a local electrician, apparently. That's how she met him. He did some work for her.'

'But you weren't convinced?'

'Must have been doing a lot of work in this street,' said Heather with a smile, 'but he was never out there when Grace was at work.'

'Can we have a look at this photo you took?'

Heather picked up her smartphone from the top of the pile of books next to her armchair. Pat wondered if the pile was going to tumble, but she steadied it with her hand before opening the photos app on her phone. 'Here it is.' She passed the device to Pat.

Pat looked at the image on the screen. It showed the rear view of a dirty white van with Snowdon Electrical barely visible through the grime and a number plate clean enough to read. He handed the device to Lina.

'You okay with me sending a copy of this to my phone?' said Lina.

'Please,' said Heather. 'I don't know if it's him you need to find, but I'll sleep easier knowing you've at least checked him out.'

'We need to have another chat with Sophie,' said Pat. 'See what you can set up with her grandmother while I look up this registration number.'

Lina sat at her desk and logged on to her computer. 'Do you want me to look back over her bank statements for a payment to Snowdon Electrical?'

'Let me confirm which Phil we're looking for first.'

'Okay, I'll see if I can get onto Mrs Williams.'

Pat waited for his computer to fire up and then keyed the registration number from Heather Fountain's photograph into the motor vehicles database. His query came back with a Phillip Edward Snowdon, aged 45, at an address on Sunderland Crescent, Seaford.

Pat switched screens and ran a search on Snowdon Electrical and got several hits. The highest rating entry was for a Facebook page, followed by a local tradesman's listing for Seaford. Pat wrote down the mobile phone number listed as the firm's contact number and then called it.

'Snowdon Electrical.'

'Is that Phillip Snowdon?' said Pat.

'No, this is Matt. Dad's out on a job, but I can help you. What do you need done?'

'Matt, this is Detective Sergeant Travers. I'd like to speak to your dad about a job he did in Moana a few months back. Do you have a number I can call him on?'

'Sure. 0418 237 986. He might not answer if he's busy, but you can always leave a message.'

'Thanks, Matt.'

Pat ended the call and keyed in the number Matt had given him.

'Phil Snowdon.'

'Phil, this is Detective Sergeant Travers. I'm investigating the death of Grace Williams. I understand you did a job for her recently at her home in Moana.'

'Yeah, I installed a couple of ceiling fans for her at the start of the summer.'

'That would mean some of the fingerprints and DNA we found in her house are probably yours, if you were there only a few months ago.'

'I guess so.'

'We're trying to narrow down the number of unidentified prints and DNA samples we have, so I'd appreciate it if you could come in and help us out with that.'

'Where do I need to come?'

'Christies Beach Police Station. It's on Beach Road.'

'Your lucky day, mate. I've just finished here. Can be there in about ten minutes, if that's okay?'

'That will be fine, Phil. Ask for me at reception when you get here.'

CHAPTER 15

Fifteen minutes after speaking to Phil Snowdon on the phone, Pat ushered a tallish man with a shaved head into an interview room at Christies Beach, thinking to himself that Phil probably worked out at one of the local gyms.

'Phil, this is Detective Constable Palumbo. She'll take your fingerprints and collect a sample of your DNA,' said Pat, 'provided you're happy to consent to giving them to help us as part of our investigation.

'No problem,' said Phil. 'Happy to help, but I do have one question.'

'Oh, what's that?'

'What happens to this stuff after you've used it?'

'That's up to you, Phil. If you consent, we can add it to the national database which could help us with future investigations, or you can ask us to destroy it once we've used it to reduce the amount of unidentified material collected from our crime scene.'

'I'd rather have it destroyed,' said Phil.

Sensible, thought Pat. 'That's okay. Just tick that box before you sign the form granting us consent to collect your samples.' Pat slid the form across the table to Phil, handed him a pen, and watched while Phil read through the form before completing it.

'What happens now?'

Pat waited while Lina explained the procedure and then collected the samples.

'Is that it?' said Phil, when Lina had finished.

'Got time for a couple of questions before you go?' said Pat. 'We're trying to fill in some of Grace's background details.'

Phil cocked an eyebrow. 'What sort of questions? I didn't know her all that well.'

'But you did know her a bit, didn't you? We've been told your van was at her place more than once over the summer.'

'Well, I did a couple of jobs for her. Installed some ceiling fans, like I said, and then she had me back just before Christmas to replace some outside lights.'

Pat leant on the doorframe of the interview room. 'Sure there wasn't more to your relationship with Grace?'

'I wish,' said Phil. 'She was real friendly and liked to talk. I got the impression she was lonely. Been a bit that way myself since the missus up and left me.' Phil shrugged. 'We went out a couple of times, but it didn't go anywhere.' Phil smiled. 'Bloke can't be blamed for trying, can he?'

'Guess not. Did you meet her daughter?'

'Sophie? Yeah. Don't think she liked me much. Always went next door when I was there.'

Pat smiled. 'Kids can be like that. When was the last time you saw Grace?'

Phil stroked his chin and then touched his nose. 'Be about six weeks ago, I suppose.'

'Do any other jobs around where she lived?'

'Most of my work comes from Moana and Seaford. Sometimes I get a job up around here or further south, but not often. That's how I got the job at Grace's. Someone she knew recommended me.'

'You said she liked to talk. Did she ever mention if she'd been threatened by anyone?'

'If she had, I'd have been here to tell you as soon as I heard she'd been killed. She didn't deserve that.'

Pat opened the door. 'Thanks for coming in, Phil. Appreciate your help.'

'Why didn't you ask him about what Grace's neighbour told us about seeing his van in the street?' said Lina, as they made their way back to the incident room.

'Let's see what his mobile phone data tells us about where he's been over the last three months or so. I want to know if he was stalking her or if his movements have been relatively random.'

'He'd have a motive if he was the possessive or jealous type,' said Lina.

'Let's see if he had an opportunity on the day Grace was killed. By the way, how did you get on with Mrs Williams?'

'We can see them on the way home this afternoon. Sophie will be home by four.'

'That works for me,' said Pat. 'Let's see what we can find out about our mate Snowdon while we're waiting. And, why don't you take a look through Grace's bank statements to see if there's a record of her payments to Snowdon Electrical?'

CHAPTER 16

Mrs Williams stepped out onto her front porch, closing the door behind her, as soon as Pat and Lina pulled into the driveway behind her car.

'This doesn't look good,' said Pat, as he opened the door to get out of the car.

Mrs Williams met them in front of their car. 'Sophie's not having a good day. Some kids at school have been giving her a hard time. She wasn't happy when I said you were coming to see her.'

'We won't keep her long,' said Pat.

'I'm not sure she'll talk to you. She gets upset any time I mention her mother,' said Mrs Williams. 'What is it you wanted to ask her about?'

'An electrician who did some work in your daughter's apartment. Phil Snowdon.'

'That dirtbag! Grace told me she thought he was a nice bloke until he tried to come on to her.'

'Any reason why you didn't mention him before?'

'Didn't occur to me. She'd told him to piss off weeks before she was killed, and it's not as if she'd been in any sort of relationship with him. At least, that's what she told me. Anyway, if you hadn't mentioned his name, I would never have thought of him.'

Dressed in her school uniform, Sophie opened the front door and stepped onto the porch. 'Are you going to come in or stay out here talking about me?'

'Guess we'd better go in, then,' said Mrs Williams, turning and walking towards the house.

―――――――

Sophie came in last and sat on the couch next to Lina. 'What do you want to ask me about?'

'What can you tell us about Phil Snowdon?' said Lina.

'Real smooth talker. Mum fell for him straightaway.' Sophie shook her head. 'I didn't like him.'

'Why was that?' said Lina.

'He's like those boys at school that come over real friendly, when all they want is to feel you up and brag about it to their mates.' She crossed her arms and legs and hunched her shoulders. 'After they've had their fun, they don't want to know you.'

'Know the type you mean,' said Lina, 'and, unfortunately, they're not all schoolboys.'

Sophie smiled and her tight pose lost some of its tension.

'We spoke to Phil this morning when we found out he'd been in your house.'

'How did you find out he'd been to our place?'

'Mrs Fountain told us.'

'Is she back?'

'Yes. I think she'd like to hear from you.'

'I must ring her,' said Sophie. 'She's really sweet.'

'Phil said your mother had him around twice to fix some stuff at your house. Is that right?'

'Yeah. He put in the ceiling fans, and then he came back to fix the light out the back.'

'Are those the only times he visited your house?'

Sophie shook her head. 'He took Mum out a couple of times. I didn't go. I stayed home with Mrs Fountain.'

'When was the last time you saw him?'

Sophie pulled her smartphone out of her pocket and scrolled through her calendar. 'Fifth of February. They went to the Beach Hotel for dinner. When she got home, Mum told me she'd told him he wasn't her type. I could have told her that, but who listens to a fifteen-year-old?'

'Did you ever see his van in the street near your house after that?'

'No, but I spend most of the day at school, don't I?'

'Any reason why you didn't mention him to us when we spoke to you before?'

Sophie shrugged. 'I didn't think he counted. Why are you so interested in him now?'

Lina looked at Pat.

'Mrs Fountain told us she had seen Phil's van parked in your street several times in the weeks before your mother was killed,' said Pat. 'In fact, she gave us a photograph of it parked in your street.'

'That would be right. Nothing happens around our place without her knowing.' Sophie smiled. 'She's a lovely old lady, but she's as nosy as hell.'

'Sometimes, nosy neighbours can be helpful when we're investigating,' said Pat, 'because they see things other people don't.'

'Guess the killer was lucky she went to Tassie,' said Sophie, 'otherwise she would have seen him.'

'No doubt,' said Lina. 'Now, is there anyone else you've forgotten to tell us about, Sophie?'

'Mum didn't go out much,' said Sophie, 'and when she did, it was usually with people from where she worked. The only place we went regularly was church, every Sunday.' Sophie raised her eyebrows. 'She even insisted I join the youth group Pastor Thomas started.'

'How's that working out now you know he's your brother?' said Lina.

Sophie shrugged. 'He's great, but some of the kids at school aren't.'

'They'll get over it,' said Lina. 'You'll be old news soon enough and they'll have something or someone else to talk about.'

'Hope you're right,' said Mrs Williams. 'Is this Phil a suspect?'

'He's a person of interest,' said Pat, 'because he was in Grace's life, even if only for a brief period. He's helped us eliminate at least one set of unidentified fingerprints.'

'Sorry I didn't mention him,' said Sophie. 'But, to be honest, he's someone I'd like to forget.'

CHAPTER 17

PAT SEARCHED through the location data for Phil Snowdon's mobile phone. The first time it had pinged a tower in the vicinity of Grace William's apartment had been on the first Monday of December, which Pat assumed was when Phil had installed the ceiling fans. In the following six weeks, the phone had pinged the same tower every Wednesday morning between nine and midday. On three of those mornings it appeared Phil had been in the vicinity for less than thirty minutes, but on the other three he'd stayed for an hour or more.

After the initial six-week period, Pat could not discern a pattern in the location data. It did reveal, however, that Phil had been near Grace's apartment twice on the fifth of February, which aligned with what Sophie had told them.

The rest of the phone location data confirmed what Phil Snowdon had told them about his business-related movements.

Pat wondered why Phil had been hanging around near Grace's apartment on the six Wednesday mornings after he'd installed her ceiling fans.

'Have a look at this, Lina,' said Pat. 'Our boy was some-where close to Grace's apartment on six consecutive Wednesday mornings after he'd installed her ceiling fans. What do you think he was up to?'

'Wednesday mornings?' said Lina. 'Isn't that when Mrs Fountain told us Alastair Holt visited Grace?'

'What would be the connection?' Pat didn't believe in coincidences. There had to be a reason why Phil Snowdon had been in the vicinity of Grace's apartment on those Wednesday mornings. 'Somebody must have known about their relationship and suspected something.'

'What do you mean?'

'Phil's an electrician. What if he'd been paid to install a listening device in Grace's apartment? That would explain why he was parked nearby on those Wednesday mornings. He was there to pick up its signal while Alastair was with Grace.'

'But didn't Grace organise the installation?' said Lina.

'We only have Phil's word for that,' said Pat. 'What do her banking records show?'

'There's only a record of her paying him on the twenty-third of December. Nothing before that, and I can't find a record of her paying for the ceiling fans either.'

'I guess she could have paid cash,' said Pat.

'I don't think she paid cash for anything,' said Lina, 'going by these statements.'

'Looks like someone's given her a Trojan horse, then,' said Pat. 'Come on, let's go see if it's still there.'

It took the CSI technician less than five minutes to locate the miniature surveillance camera hidden within the ceiling fan housing in Grace's bedroom. To the naked eye of anyone standing on the floor, it looked like a screw holding the housing's cover in place, until the technician removed it and held it out for Pat to see.

'I'll need to measure the strength of the signal,' said the technician, 'but these things have a range out to fifty metres or more.'

'Our man was parked in the street a couple of houses back,' said Pat.

'He would have been in range.'

'What would he need to pick up the signal?'

'A smartphone with the right app would do the trick. He'd only have to pair it with the camera when he installed it.'

'Let me know if you manage to lift any prints,' said Pat. 'We have our suspect's on file.'

CHAPTER 18

THIS PLACE'S overdue for a revamp, thought Pat, as he entered the interview room they'd been assigned and took his seat opposite Phil Snowdon and his lawyer. The decor was dated, the walls a depressing grey matched with a carpet of an indistinct colour that might once have held a checked pattern. All the carpet held now was the lingering odour of too many unwashed bodies sweating under pressure. He waited while Lina fiddled with the AV equipment and then walked those present through the required introductory protocols.

Phil Snowdon scowled as he spat out his name for the recording, and Pat wondered if Phil thought he could intimidate him. He knew from his research that Phil had never been held to account for his illegal surveillance activities, at least not in South Australia, so it was possible he'd never been formally interviewed in relation to a crime before and really didn't know how to respond to being arrested. Perhaps his tough exterior was a mask hiding his fear.

'Accessory to murder is a serious charge, Phil,' said Pat. 'You're looking at some serious time inside.'

'I didn't kill anyone.'

'I'm not saying you did,' said Pat, 'but, from where I'm sitting, it looks like you helped someone who did.'

'What do you mean?'

They always act ignorant to the facts, thought Pat, even when they know perfectly well what they've done. 'How about you tell us how you got the job installing those ceiling fans for Grace Williams?'

'Like I told you before, she called me and booked the job.'

That aligned with Grace's call log, so Phil was telling the truth so far, thought Pat. 'Did you supply the fans or had she already purchased them?'

Phil shrugged. 'I don't remember.'

Pat lowered his rating of Phil's willingness to tell them the truth. 'That would be on your invoice for the job, wouldn't it?'

'If there was an invoice,' said Phil.

'Are you saying there might not be an invoice?'

Phil looked at his lawyer. 'Not if she paid cash.'

'I'm not the tax office, Phil, and going by what I've seen of your books, I doubt it would be worth their while for me to report you for not keeping proper records. What does interest me, though, is there is no record of your transaction with Grace Williams. Not in your books, and not in her bank records.'

'That's because she paid cash.'

Pat doubted that. According to Grace's bank statements, she rarely paid cash for anything and there had been no significant cash withdrawal from her account around the time of the installation of the fans, which left Pat wondering who had paid for the fans and their installation.

'You haven't taken your son into your confidences, have you?'

'What's that supposed to mean?'

'He seems to think you're running a legitimate business.'

'I am.'

'You might have the appropriate licence to install security cameras, Phil, but, as far as I can establish, you're not licensed to conduct covert surveillance or to record private conversations in this state, are you?'

'Why would I have to be?'

Pat opened his folder and held up the transparent evidence bag holding the miniature camera they'd retrieved from Grace Williams' apartment. 'This is why you're here. This is a pretty sophisticated piece of kit. You know what this is, don't you?'

Phil said nothing.

'That's a question, Mr Snowdon,' said Lina. 'You need to answer it.'

'No comment.'

Pat showed the bag to the lawyer. 'This is a miniature camera retrieved from a ceiling fan your client installed in Grace Williams' apartment. The camera bit is tiny, almost invisible when in place, but the transmitter unit is large enough for your client to have left a fingerprint on it.' Pat turned his focus back to Phil Snowdon. 'You'd be looking at three years or a fifteen thousand dollar fine for installing this, Phil, if that was your only offence.'

Pat put the evidence bag on top of his folder where Phil could see it. 'Want to tell us who asked you to install this camera and monitor its signal?'

'I don't know,' said Phil. 'Look, I admit I installed it, but this work comes through a broker. It's all anonymous and they pay cash.'

I bet they do, thought Pat. 'How do they contact you?'

'I get a letter telling me where to pick up the instructions and the money.'

'A letter? In this day and age?'

'No digital footprint,' said Phil. 'They're not idiots.'

'Still have that letter or those instructions?'

'No. I'm not that stupid.'

You were stupid enough not to wear gloves when handling the camera, thought Pat, wondering if he could get Phil to make any more mistakes. 'What did the instructions say for the job involving Grace?'

'To wait for her to call me and then to monitor the signal until they got what they wanted. They already knew their target only visited her on Wednesday mornings.'

'Did they tell you who the target was?'

'No, but it wasn't hard to work out.'

'So, you knew it was Alastair Holt?'

'Yeah.'

'What did you do with the recordings?'

'Saved them to a USB and dropped them where they told me to leave them.'

'And where was that?'

'At the Uniting Church Cemetery on Seaford Road. Under the fifth cypress pine on the right-hand side of the path leading down to the pavilion.'

'Really?' said Pat. 'You expect me to believe you left it in a public space where anybody could have picked it up without verifying you'd given it to the correct person?'

'The only person who knew it was there was whoever paid for it.'

'How did they know it was there?'

'Haven't you ever watched a James Bond movie, mate? They set a date and a time, and they probably had someone watching me make the delivery.'

'When did you make this delivery?'

'Eleven o'clock on the night of the eighteenth of January.'

'Was there a final payment?'

'Yeah, the client was happy, so I got paid.'

'How was that made?'

Phil smiled. 'Australia Post.'

Smart-arse, thought Pat. 'Why didn't you say something when your target was killed?'

'Do you think I wanted to put a target on my back?'

'What about when Grace was killed? I thought you liked her.'

'What was I going to tell you? I didn't know who I was working for. Still don't.'

Pat slipped the evidence bag back into his folder. 'Still makes you an accessory, Phil.'

'I thought they only wanted to destroy the bastard's reputation. You ever heard him preach? Prick was a real hypocrite.' Phil looked at his hands. 'I didn't know they were going to kill him and Grace. If I'd known that, I wouldn't have done it.'

'Yeah, well, you're going to have to live with that, regardless of what the court decides.'

'What do you think?' said Pat, as he and Lina made their way back to the incident room after interviewing Phil Snowdon.

'We're probably too late to go through his rubbish

looking for any traces of the letter he mentioned or the packaging the money came in.'

'Let's go through his phone records again and see if there are any numbers that show up regularly, or just before the installation and around the eighteenth of January.'

'You don't believe him about the letter?'

'No, and get Forensics to have a go at getting into his phone to see if he's using any encrypted messaging apps.'

'Okay. Do you think Sophie might know where the fans came from?'

'She seems to trust you. Why don't you give her a call after school?' said Pat. 'Let's grab a coffee and then have another chat with Heather Fountain. Somebody has to have let the cat out of the bag about Alastair being at Grace's on Wednesday mornings, and she's as good a source as any I can think of, even if she did it unintentionally.'

Pat's phone vibrated in his pocket.

'DS Travers.'

'You making any progress on that case you're working on, Pat,' said DI Smith. 'I've got the media badgering me for an update.'

Pat realised he hadn't checked in with the boss since they'd arrested Snowdon. 'Sorry, Boss. Snowdon's confessed to doing the surveillance on Holt but claims he doesn't know who commissioned the job.'

'Why didn't he come forward when he heard Holt had been killed?'

'Probably for the same reason he's not being honest with us now,' said Pat. 'He doesn't want to get himself killed.'

'So, what are you doing now?'

'We're trying to find out where the ceiling fans came from. Snowdon says he didn't supply them and we can't find a record of Grace Williams having bought them, so I'm assuming someone gifted them to her and recommended Snowdon for the installation.'

'Sounds like you're dealing with someone who planned this down to the tee, Pat,' said DI Smith. 'Keep me in the loop.'

CHAPTER 19

'That's an interesting question, Sergeant,' said Heather. 'I could have told any number of people.'

'Can you recall anyone in particular?' said Pat.

Heather lifted the cup from her kitchen table to her lips and took a sip of tea. 'I remember talking about how impressed I was by his regular pastoral visits with some women Grace introduced me to at their church. They were a nosy lot. Wanted to know why I'd come with Grace.' She took another sip of her tea and then put the cup back into its saucer on the table. 'But that was a couple of years ago. I haven't seen any of them since.'

'Do you remember any of their names?'

'Not really. They were members of some sort of women's group Grace belonged to. Sophie might know who some of them are. She was with us.'

That sounded promising to Pat, but he wondered if Heather had spoken to anyone about Alastair's visits more recently.

'Can you think of anyone you caught up with in the last

few months of last year that you might have mentioned his visits to?'

Heather crossed her arms and frowned. 'Probus. We meet on the first Monday of every month in the Sports Centre at Reynella. That would have to be it.' She leant back in her chair. 'We had a guest speaker in October last year, a social worker. He talked about the value of visiting older people in their homes and specifically mentioned how the declining number of priests was making it even more important for members of the community to get involved. I remember telling the people at my table about how my neighbour's pastor visited her every week.'

'Do you remember their names?'

Heather shook her head. 'At our age, Sergeant, we need a name tag every time we meet, and people usually only put their first name on the tag. But, the people at my table were all women. One of them was my friend, Martha Hartwood. She's on her own, like me. We taught together at Woodcroft and often go on holidays together. We've just been to Tasmania. Oh, I think I told you that before.' She looked at Pat and smiled. 'You could get the names of the others from the secretary. I suppose. I can give you her number.'

'That would be good.'

Heather scrolled through her contacts, found the number, and read it out while Lina wrote it down in her notebook. 'How do you think that will help?'

Pat smiled. 'I'm assuming you didn't arrange the hit on Pastor Holt or your neighbour, Mrs Fountain. Would that be a safe assumption?'

Heather looked horrified. 'You couldn't possibly think I had anything to do with their murders, could you?'

Pat held up his hands in front of him. 'Of course not.

Where you come in, Mrs Fountain, is you're one of the few people who knew Alastair visited Grace every Wednesday morning. Not even his wife knew that. What I'm hoping is knowing who you told about it will lead us to someone who had a reason to kill them.'

'Would hardly think the people I know in Probus would do that.'

'Maybe so,' said Pat, 'but it's that six degrees of separation thing. We're all only six social connections away from anyone else.'

'It would have to be someone in that church, wouldn't it?'

'Possibly,' said Pat. 'I guess time will tell.' He got up from the table. 'Grace didn't, by any chance, tell you where she got her new ceiling fans from, did she?'

'She said they were an early Christmas present, but she never said who from. I assumed her parents had bought them. They were always helping her out.'

Lina called Sophie Williams at the end of her shift.

'Hi, Sophie. It's Lina Palumbo. Got a minute?'

'I suppose.'

Lina wondered whether Sophie's tone was a teenage girl thing or a sign she was reluctant to engage with her. 'Do you remember who your mother got the new ceiling fans from? She told Mrs Fountain they were an early Christmas present.'

'Pastor Holt got them for us. Mum said we couldn't afford new ones.'

'Do you know if Pastor Holt gave them to her himself, or did he only arrange for you to get them?'

'I don't know. All I remember is we picked them up from church and Mum rang Phil to come around and put them in. She said if we used him we wouldn't have to pay for it,' said Sophie. 'Why do you want to know?'

'We've arrested Phil,' said Lina. 'He attached a surveillance camera to the fan in your mother's bedroom.'

'Why?'

'Someone wanted to know what Pastor Holt was doing at your mother's place every Wednesday.'

There was a moment's silence, as if Sophie were processing that piece of information.

'I just knew Phil was a sicko!'

'I'm so sorry you had to go through that,' said Lina.

'Was there a camera in my room? Was he perving on me, too?'

'No,' said Lina. 'I had the technician check. There was only the one camera in your mother's room.'

'That's disgusting,' said Sophie. 'Who would want to spy on them?'

'I don't know yet, but we're working on finding out.'

'I hope you do,' said Sophie. 'I don't know who to trust anymore.'

'You can trust me,' said Lina. 'I won't lie to you.'

'I hope so,' said Sophie.

'Is your grandmother there?' said Lina. 'I'd like a quick word with her.'

'She's just here. I'll give her the phone.'

Lina listened as Sophie explained to her grandmother who was on the phone.

'Hello?'

'Mrs Williams, Lina Palumbo. Just wanted to let you know we've arrested Phil Snowdon.'

'Did he kill her?'

'We don't think so, but we know he put a surveillance camera in Grace's bedroom and passed on the recording to someone else.'

'Who?'

'We don't know yet, but we think whoever it was, they somehow knew about the gift of the ceiling fans.'

'That doesn't make any sense, Lina. She told me Alastair got them for her for Christmas.'

'Obviously someone else must have known,' said Lina, 'because they used that gift to collect the evidence confirming their relationship.'

'Well, it wasn't me,' said Mrs Williams. 'I've known about it since she got pregnant with Sophie.'

Lina almost dropped her phone. She hadn't expected that. 'And you didn't think to say anything?'

'She swore me to secrecy. Not even her father knew until you told us.'

Lina took a deep breath. The woman could have saved them time if she'd volunteered what she knew about her daughter's relationship earlier, but Lina realised there was little to be gained by upbraiding her for her failure to do so. She needed to keep Mrs Williams onside in case she needed more from Sophie.

'You're an amazing mother, Mrs Williams. I can't imagine my mother being able to keep a secret like that.'

'You do what you have to do so you don't lose them,' said Mrs Williams, 'not that it helped in the end.'

CHAPTER 20

In the days after receiving news of Alastair's indiscretion from Thomas, the Council of Elders worked the phones to elicit as much community input as they could before making their decision final.

They discovered the community was divided. The older members, who had supported the church for years, were furious at Alastair's betrayal of his own preaching. Several older members, tarring Thomas with the same brush, demanded the immediate termination of Thomas' appointment as pastor. Others, expressing a dislike for his style of preaching, urged the elders to fire him and engage a more traditional preacher, someone who not only preached like Alastair but also lived up to his preaching.

The younger members of the community were more forgiving. Their children liked Pastor Thomas. But they were in the minority and hadn't made the same financial contribution as the older cohort of members, who had sacrificed to establish the community.

As word spread, Reg was approached by Pastor Brian

Reynolds, the recently retired senior pastor of a neigh-
bouring community church, with an offer to serve as their
interim pastor for the next five years. When Reg presented
Pastor Reynolds' offer to the Council of Elders, he pitched it
as a circuit breaker that would allow the community to move
on from the fallout of the scandal.

'Sounds like the perfect solution to our problem,' said
Michael.

'Yes, and he's available to start straight away,' said Henry.

'I think we're making a mistake,' said Sam. 'Thomas has
the makings of a great pastor.'

'We need to make a decision that reflects the view of
most members,' said Reg. 'They want a clean cut from what
Alastair did to them. They don't want to take the risk of
Thomas being like his father.'

'But we know he's not,' said Sam.

'It's all about perception,' said Henry. 'We're not saying
Thomas has done anything wrong, but he's followed in his
father's footsteps before. Who's to know if he won't do it
again?'

'That's a bit harsh, isn't it?' said Sam.

'Not a risk we want to take,' said Reg. 'We're lucky Brian
Reynolds is available to start with us immediately. He has an
impeccable record and comes highly recommended. I've
spoken to the chairman of their Council of Elders.'

'This could divide the community,' said Sam. 'The
younger ones really like Thomas.'

'It comes down to who pays to keep the community
running,' said Henry, 'and that's not the young ones. It's the
people that have been prepared to put their hands into their
pockets again and again, and they've told us they don't want

Thomas as their pastor after this. He's too much of a reminder of the scandal Alastair brought down on us.'

'So be it,' said Sam. 'Who am I to stand in the way of the community's decision?' He looked across the table at Reg. 'Best to record it in the minutes as being unanimous.'

Thomas stood outside the door to the meeting room at the back of the church, attempting to settle the butterflies in his stomach into a stable formation. The elders had summoned him to their meeting without sending him a copy of their agenda, and he'd heard from several community members that they'd been canvassing people's opinions on what they should do in response to the public disclosure of Alastair's affair with Grace.

Thomas wiped his hands on his trousers, knocked, and opened the door. Four heads turned to face him as he entered the room and took his seat at the near end of the table. 'I hope you weren't expecting me to prepare anything. I didn't get an agenda.'

'This is an extraordinary meeting,' said Reg. 'There is only one item of business.'

'Oh, and what's that?' said Thomas, looking at the glum faces around the table and wondering if someone had died.

'You've no doubt heard we've been consulting with the community about what they want us to do in light of the news of Alastair's relationship with Grace Williams,' said Reg, without looking directly at Thomas.

'I have,' said Thomas, losing control of his butterfly formation.

Reg picked up an envelope from the table in front of him and handed it across the table to Thomas. 'This is your letter of termination, Thomas. The community has decided it doesn't want you to continue as their pastor. Their decision is effective immediately. We're giving you four weeks' pay instead of notice and we want you out of the house by the end of the month.'

Thomas looked at the other three elders seated around the table. They were looking at the tabletop. 'I've dedicated the last few years of my life to serving this community. What have I done to let you down?'

'You haven't done anything wrong,' said Sam. 'It's not about you.'

'I'm being punished for the sins of my father. Is that it?'

'That's the community's decision, I'm afraid,' said Reg. 'No-one wants to run the risk of you turning out to be like your father. That would be the end of us.'

'Seems I must have misjudged this community, then,' said Thomas. 'Sounds like you're a reflection of my father's preaching, after all.'

'We created this community,' said Reg, 'and we'll see it survive and prosper under the guidance of a pastor who sees things our way.'

Thomas wondered if their beliefs reflected his father's preaching or whether his father's preaching had actually reflected their shared beliefs. 'And who would that be?'

'Pastor Brian Reynolds,' said Reg. 'He's accepted our invitation to shepherd the community in the style we prefer until we find a suitable replacement.'

Thomas had met Brian Reynolds. He was old-fashioned like his father and nearly as old. 'So, you don't like my style of preaching?'

'That's the message we're getting,' said Reg. 'We've nothing against you, Thomas. I'm sure you'll make a great preacher somewhere, but not here.'

'Will I get the opportunity to say goodbye to the community on Sunday?'

Reg looked around the table at the others. 'We suggest you keep your goodbyes informal, Thomas. We don't want any scenes.'

There must be a few members who want me to stay, thought Thomas, as he stood to leave the meeting. That meant he'd got through to some of them in the short time he'd been in the community. 'Thanks for the opportunity to see what it was like to work as a pastor. I hope things work out for you with Brian Reynolds.'

Thomas stuffed his termination letter into his trouser pocket and left the room, closing the door quietly behind him.

Thomas was relieved he'd handled his dismissal without losing it with the Council of Elders. Inside, he'd been burning with anger at the unfairness of being dismissed because of the actions of his father, yet he'd managed to stay calm and keep his dignity.

Their reasoning had been eye-opening for him. He'd thought he was going to introduce the community to a more inclusive set of gospel values but, apparently, that's not what most of them wanted to hear. Maybe, he thought, the elders were doing him a favour by firing him as their pastor. His termination certainly meant he'd avoid all the frustration he now knew he would have felt if they'd allowed him to stay on and try to open their hearts to the message he wanted to preach.

As he walked across the yard to the house he was being evicted from at the end of the month, he wondered how the members of the community who had embraced him as their pastor would respond to the news he'd been fired. Several members had sympathised with him after his father's relationship with Grace had become common knowledge. He knew he was popular with the kids, especially the teens. They wouldn't be happy when they found out.

He wondered what had really driven the elders to make the decision they'd made, since no-one had complained to his face about his preaching. It had to be their deep-seated sense of betrayal by Alastair. He knew they were members of the founding families of the community. His father had told him the story of how his grandfather and his friends had started the church often enough. Perhaps, he thought, as he flopped down into the armchair that had once been his father's favourite chair, he'd have to start a church of his own if he wanted to continue as a pastor. But, for now, he needed to tell someone he'd lost his job.

He pulled out his phone and called Marianne.

'How did the meeting go?'

'They sacked me, Mum. Effective immediately.'

'Why? What have they accused you of doing?'

'Their official line is the community doesn't like my preaching style, but it's really about them punishing me for Dad's sins. They don't want to run the risk of me turning out like him.'

'That's not fair!'

'What's fairness got to do with anything, Mum? Do you think what Dad did was fair?'

Thomas heard Marianne take a deep breath and realised she was doing her best not to cry. 'Maybe it's for the best, Mum.'

'What are you going to do?'

'I don't know yet, but I'm going to need to find somewhere to live while I sort that out. They've only given me to the end of the month to be out of here.'

'That's only ten days,' said Marianne. 'Why don't you come and stay with me while you sort things out? I've got plenty of room and you'll need somewhere to store your tools.'

'Are you sure?'

'Who else is going to look after you rent free while you get back on your feet or find another community looking for a progressive young pastor?'

'You're an angel, Mum.'

'Why don't you come over now for tea and we can talk about it?'

'Thanks, Mum. See you shortly.'

Thomas fell back into the depth of the armchair. He closed his eyes. It was the end of an era. He'd lived his entire life in this house next to the church on the outskirts of McLaren Vale, except for the years he'd spent at Trinity College in Melbourne studying to become a pastor.

He opened his eyes and looked around the room at the few items of furniture that had been left in the house when his parents had moved to the house they'd purchased for their retirement. He shook his head. What had he been thinking? This was his father's world, and it felt as fraudulent as his father had been. These people weren't interested in gospel values like love and forgiveness. They were only interested in being right. He needed to find a community with open hearts and minds or find something else to do with his life.

He hoped his mother would understand if he decided to leave in search of his dream.

CHAPTER 21

'PAT!'

Angela touched his arm. Pat blinked. He'd been deep in a field of floating thoughts, searching for a way to connect the pieces of his puzzle into a coherent picture. 'What?'

'Are you always this distracted when you're working on a case? That's the third time I've called you.'

'Sorry.' He smiled, and let her pull him up from the armchair he'd been sitting in while she'd been fussing over the finishing touches to the meal she was preparing for them. 'Shutting it all out is not always easy, especially when I'm not doing something else. I find myself going down rabbit holes looking for answers.'

'Find anything this time?' Angela laughed. She obviously wasn't expecting an answer. 'Come on, food's ready. Can you open the wine?' She led him into the dining room.

Pat cracked the screw top on the Pinot Noir and poured the wine into their glasses. Having dinner with Angela on a Friday night was becoming a regular thing. Tonight she'd made veal parmigiana accompanied by spaghetti with marinara sauce.

'Hope that's enough for you. We can't have you putting on weight.'

'The jogging's keeping that in check.'

'You're looking a lot healthier,' said Angela. 'Something must be working for you.'

'Feeling a lot better, too,' said Pat.

'Funny how having someone special in your life does that.' Angela smiled, leant across the table, and squeezed his hand. 'Thanks for showing up when you did.'

'We have Lina to thank for that,' said Pat. 'Have to admit I'd never thought of her as a matchmaker.' He laughed.

'Think my sister might have had something to do with it,' said Angela, slicing her veal into edible chunks.

'Well, here's to them,' said Pat, picking up his glass.

'I'll drink to that,' said Angela, clinking glasses with him. 'How's your Mum?'

'She's good. I'm taking her out to lunch with Rose and Martin on Sunday. It's Martin's birthday.'

'That should be good. Going anywhere special?'

'Rose has made a booking somewhere on Jetty Road.' Pat pushed his plate back. 'That was good.'

'You're lucky my mother was a wonderful teacher. She's a superb cook.'

Pat was still waiting to meet Angela's mother. 'What are the boys doing tonight?'

'Tony's gone to Melbourne to spend the weekend with Tiffany. Think they might be getting serious.'

'How do you feel about that?'

'He's twenty-five, Pat. It's about time he found himself someone, if you ask me.'

'And, Carlo?'

'He's gone to Moonta with my parents for one of my father's fishing expeditions. Won't be back until after lunch on Sunday.'

'So, you're home alone. What are you planning on doing?'

Angela drained her glass and held it out for a refill. 'I was hoping to spend some quality time with the new man in my life.'

Pat filled her glass and then leant across the table to kiss her. 'I think that can be arranged.'

Pressure on the bladder interrupted Pat's slumber. It took him a moment to realise he was not in his own bed and that the person snoring softly beside him was Angela. His mind went back to the lovemaking that had started tentatively between them, before erupting with passion. It had been years since he'd had sex with anyone, and he was glad he'd allowed himself to be seduced. He hoped Angela had felt as satisfied as he had before falling asleep.

Pat eased himself out of the bed and silently made his way across the carpet to the en suite. He closed the door softly and switched on the light, only to be confronted by a naked man staring at him from the mirror. He acknowledged his reflection with a half-hearted wave of his right hand and then emptied his bladder against the inside of the toilet bowl, before pushing the button on the cistern and hoping the sound of the flush wasn't loud enough to disturb Angela from her sleep.

He switched off the light and opened the door, then

stood in the doorway and waited for his eyes to adjust to the dim light of the bedroom before making his way back to bed. As he slipped back into the bed, Angela nuzzled up beside him and he felt her hand slide down his belly and caress his flaccid penis, which responded to her touch.

'Think you can go again, lover boy?'

CHAPTER 22

MONDAY MORNING. Pat had spent the weekend up to lunchtime on Sunday with Angela, when he'd joined Rose and his mother to celebrate Martin's birthday. After the years of celibacy following Pam's illness and death, he'd been nervous about making love with Angela, but once they'd crossed the initial threshold, it had seemed the most natural thing in the world to be doing. He felt invigorated as he strode across the car park and into the building.

Outside the door to the squad room, he stopped and took a couple of deep breaths, and told himself to calm down. He didn't want the spring in his step or the smile on his face to advertise how he'd spent the weekend. He knew Lina wouldn't give him a moment's peace once she realised he'd finally succumbed to her aunt's seductive intentions. And she'd be the hardest to hide it from.

Pat sat at his desk, logged on, and skimmed through his inbox. There was nothing he felt a need to get excited about. He checked his watch. It was eight fifteen. They were due in DI Smith's office at eight thirty. He wondered what was keeping Lina. It wasn't like her to be late. He checked his phone in case he hadn't heard a message from her arriving. Nothing.

He was about to send Lina a text when she walked in. 'Sorry, had to get the RAA out to start my car.'

'Flat battery?'

'Flat? No, it was dead. Cost me nearly four hundred dollars for a new one.'

'How long had you had the old one?'

'Came with the car when I bought it. That would make it four years.'

'Not bad,' said Pat, standing and putting on his suit coat. 'Come on, the boss is expecting us.'

DI Smith signalled for them to sit. They sat on the chairs in front of his desk and waited until he looked up from whatever it was he was typing.

'Do you two have any good news for me?'

'We've got a line of inquiry we're hoping will lead us to who's behind both murders,' said Pat.

'Which is?'

'We know someone arranged for Phil Snowdon to install a surveillance camera in Williams' apartment. He claims they wanted dirt on Holt, but he's not saying who. Reckons he got the job through some anonymous broker using Australia Post and that he passed the data on through a designated drop site.'

'You believe him?'

'Not completely, but it might not matter. Sophie Williams told us the ceiling fans were a gift arranged through their church by Alastair Holt.'

'I hope you're not suggesting Holt arranged for the secret recording of him having sex with Williams.'

Stranger things have happened, thought Pat, but he shook his head. 'No. I'm not suggesting that, not at all. Thought hadn't crossed my mind, to be honest. No, from what we've been told, there are at least three people who knew about Holt's regular visits to Williams.' He started counting them off on his fingers. 'Her mother. She even knew about him being Sophie's father. Then there's Dorothy Stein, who was also having a clandestine relationship with Holt. She's gone into hiding.'

'And the third person?'

'Heather Fountain. She's been Williams' next-door neighbour for the last five years. In fact, she's the only person in that street who was usually home on the Wednesday mornings when Holt visited Williams.'

'Wasn't she killed on a Wednesday morning?'

Pat could almost see the cogs twirling in DI Smith's expression. 'Yes, but Heather Fountain was in Tasmania that week.'

'Hmmm,' said DI Smith. 'Sounds like the killer must have known that.'

'We've got a few dots to join,' said Pat, 'but I think finding out who knew Heather Fountain would be away and Williams would be home on that Wednesday morning might be a good starting point.'

DI Smith crossed his arms. 'Do you have a clear motive for either murder?'

Pat shook his head. 'Dorothy Stein thought the church elders might be behind the killings, but we've yet to establish any connections.'

'Damage control? Makes sense, I suppose, but a bit risky, don't you think?'

'Not if they get away with it.'

'Who else would care about their relationship?'

'You mean, apart from his wife and son?'

'Do you still consider them persons of interest?'

'We can't place them at the murder scene of either victim at the time of death,' said Pat, 'but I guess that doesn't rule out the possibility of them having arranged the murders. They have admitted that living with him wasn't always easy.'

'Find out who knew about the fans before they were installed. Check with the church. They probably have a committee that oversees their spending,' said DI Smith, scratching his chin. 'And find out if Snowdon has done any work for them in the past. Someone had to have suggested they use him to install the fans if what he told you is correct.' DI Smith looked at his watch. 'Right, get on with it. Keep me posted.' He waved them out of his office.

CHAPTER 23

LINA PARKED in front of the address Martha Hartwood had given her. The house, a narrow-fronted courtyard home with a tiny front garden filled with rose bushes, reminded Lina of her own place. As she walked up the driveway to the front door, she wondered how Pat was getting on with his analysis of Phil Snowdon's business records. She hoped he was making more sense of them than she had.

She rang the doorbell and waited. After a few moments, the door opened, and she was looking at a grey-haired woman wearing an open-necked summer frock featuring pink roses on a black background.

'Mrs Hartwood?'

'Yes.'

'Detective Constable Lina Palumbo.' Lina held out her ID. 'We spoke earlier.'

'Oh, I've been expecting you.' Mrs Hartwood held the door open. 'Come in.'

They sat in the front room, where the carpet, the curtains, and every piece of furniture was a different shade of pink.

'Thank you for agreeing to see me,' said Lina, doing her best to focus on the black of Mrs Hartwood's dress, in an effort to stop herself from drowning in the all-encompassing sea of pink around her. 'As I mentioned, I understand you're a friend of Heather Fountain's.'

'Oh, we go way back. Taught together at Woodcroft for years before we retired. We've just come back from a holiday in Tasmania. Have you been? Fantastic scenery. Everything's so green.'

'Still on my bucket list, I'm afraid.'

'But I guess you're not here to talk about that.'

Lina took that as her sign to get down to business 'As I mentioned when I called, I'm investigating the death of Heather's next-door neighbour, Grace Williams.'

'That was dreadful. Imagine if we hadn't gone to Tasmania. Heather would have been home when it happened.'

'The fact she wasn't home is what I want to talk about.'

'Oh, why's that?'

'It turns out Heather and Grace were the only people usually home on a Wednesday morning in that whole street.'

'And you think her killer knew Heather wouldn't be home that Wednesday?'

Sharp, thought Lina. 'That's the possibility I'm investigating.'

'How do you think I can help you with that?'

'Have you heard of the idea of six degrees of separation? It's about how we're connected to almost anybody else through our friendship connections.'

'Oh yes, people say Adelaide's like that all the time. You can't go anywhere without bumping into someone you know.'

True, thought Lina. 'Heather told me she'd let very few

people know when she was going to Tasmania. She'd told Grace, and, obviously, you knew. Can you remember who you might have told when you were going on your trip?'

'I told my son, of course. He likes to know where I am, and all our friends at Probus knew. We'd talked about it for months.'

That didn't sound promising to Lina. It meant she might have to interview the members of their Probus club. Then she recalled the thought that had popped into her head when Heather had given her Martha Hartwood's name. 'Are you related to Reg Hartwood from McLaren Vale, by any chance?'

'He's my brother-in-law. I was married to his brother, David.'

Lina had checked. She knew Martha Hartwood's name wasn't on the list of members of the Southern Vales Community Church that Thomas Holt had given them. 'You aren't a member of his community church, though, are you?'

'No. I'm Anglican. Reg did try to get us to join, though, when they started that church, but that was years ago.'

Lina flicked through her notebook until she found the notes she'd recorded when they'd interviewed Heather Fountain. 'Were you at the Probus meeting in October last year when there was a guest speaker who talked about the importance of visiting older people in their homes?'

'Yes, it was the only time I'd heard someone say something positive about Alastair as a pastor, well, someone apart from Reg, who thought the sun shone out of his backside.'

'You didn't think highly of him?'

'He was full of self-righteous nonsense. Liked nothing more than telling people how to live their lives.' Mrs Hartwood smiled. 'It had never occurred to me that there was more to him until Heather told us about his weekly pastoral care visits to her neighbour. Not that it did him any good in the end.'

'Ever mention that to anyone?'

Mrs Hartwood screwed up her face. 'I had lunch with Megan. She's Reg's wife. We get on even if the boys didn't. Anyway, I had lunch with her not long after that meeting. I remember she was as surprised as I was when I told her what Heather had said about Alastair's pastoral visits to Grace. Apparently, Grace's husband died over twenty years ago and she was a regular at their weekly services.'

Lina felt a ripple of excitement. 'Did Megan know about your trip to Tasmania?'

'Oh, yes. We tried to talk her into coming with us. A holiday would do her good, but she's too much of a home-body. Doesn't like to travel.'

Lina closed her notebook. 'You've been very helpful, Mrs Hartwood. Thank you for your time.' She stood and allowed Mrs Hartwood to let her out of the house.

When she got into her car, she took out her phone and called Pat, impatient to tell him she'd found what sounded like the link back to the church elders they were looking for. He didn't pick up. She left him a message to call her and headed back to the incident room at Christies Beach.

Twenty minutes later, Lina pulled into the car park at Christies Beach in time to witness an ambulance departing from the station's main entrance with its lights flashing and siren blaring. She got out of her car and made her way towards the building, wondering what had happened. She hadn't heard any chatter on the radio about an incident at the station.

When she entered the station, the desk sergeant beckoned her over to the front desk. 'That was your sergeant going off in that ambulance. Collapsed at his desk. Heart attack by the sound of it.'

Lina put her right hand out to steady herself against the desk. 'Shit! Where are they taking him?'

'Flinders.'

'I'd better call his daughter.'

'You might want to call your boss, too,' said the desk sergeant.

'Will do.' After I call Zia Angela, thought Lina, as she headed into the incident room.

She didn't have Rose's number listed in her phone contacts, but she remembered Pat saying she taught at Brighton Primary School. She looked up the school's number and then tapped the sequence of digits on her phone's keypad.

'Brighton Primary, this is Amanda. How can I help you?'

'Hi, Amanda. I need to speak to Rose Travers.'

'She's teaching right now. Can I get her to call you back later?'

'It's a bit more urgent than that, I'm afraid. Look, my name is Lina Palumbo. I work with her father.'

'Her father's a policeman, isn't he? Has something happened to him?'

'Yes. Can you please tell Rose her father's just been taken to Flinders in an ambulance? I'm not sure what happened, but my colleagues think he might have had a heart attack. She'll want to be with him.'

'What was your name again?'

'Lina Palumbo. Rose will know who I am.'

'Can I have a number she can call you back on?'

Lina gave Amanda her mobile number.

'I'll go and tell her right away,' said Amanda.

'Thanks.'

Lina ended the call and found her contact listing for Angela.

'Romeo and Associates.'

'Carla, it's Lina. Can you put me through to Angela?'

'She's with a client.'

'Ask her to call me as soon as she's free.'

'Is something wrong, Lina?'

There's no putting anything past Carla, thought Lina. She had been Angela's personal assistant for years and Lina had never encountered anybody with a more sensitive antenna. 'It's Pat. They've just taken him to hospital. They're saying he's had a heart attack.'

'Oh, shit!' said Carla. 'Angela's only just finished telling me what a wonderful weekend she had with him.'

Life sucks sometimes, thought Lina. 'Tell her I'll call her as soon as I have more news.'

'You take care now, Lina.'

Lina ended the call and scrolled through her contacts until she found DI Paul Smith's number.

'What's up, Lina?'

'Afraid I've got some bad news, Inspector. Pat collapsed at his desk while I was in the field. He's been taken to Flinders. Word is they think he's had a heart attack.'

'That's not good. Have you told anyone else?'

'I've alerted his daughter.'

'Good, and how are you? Are you okay?'

Keep it professional, Lina heard the voice in her head advise. 'I'm fine. I wasn't here when it happened.'

'People survive heart attacks these days, Lina. Pat's a fighter.'

'I hope you're right, sir.'

'You'll need to step up and run the investigation in his absence, at least until I find someone to cover for him. Think you can do that for me?'

'That shouldn't be a problem, sir.'

'Thanks for letting me know. If there's anything you need, call me. Are you sure you're okay?'

'I'll be fine, sir.'

'Stay in touch.' The inspector ended the call.

Lina sat back in her chair and stared out the window at the clear blue sky. What was she going to do if Pat didn't survive?

CHAPTER 24

LINA DECIDED to stay in the incident room at Christies Beach and keep herself busy, while she waited to find out about how Pat was doing. Hearing his condition had deteriorated wasn't something she wanted to deal with in public.

She fluffed around for a while with the contents of her inbox in an attempt to distract herself. Then she turned her attention to what Pat had been looking for when she'd gone to interview Martha Hartwood.

She knew Phil Snowdon's business records were incomplete. He'd told them he didn't issue invoices for cash jobs, so it was possible he'd done a job for someone connected to the Southern Vales Community Church without making a record of it. As she scrolled through his bank statements, she hoped someone had asked for an invoice and insisted on paying electronically.

After studying several pages, the transaction she was looking for appeared at the top of the next page she opened to examine. A deposit entry with a six-digit reference number, dated in March of the previous year and listing a two thousand five hundred and sixty-dollar payment made from an account labelled as SVCC Maintenance. Lina rubbed her eyes with her fingers. She'd nearly missed it.

She opened her notebook and started making a list of the signs pointing to the involvement of someone connected to the church. Someone had requested covert surveillance of their pastor, Alastair Holt. That surveillance had been carried out by Phil Snowdon, using a miniature camera he'd installed within a ceiling fan the church had allegedly supplied to Grace Williams. Since Snowdon had obviously done a job for the church, he had to be known by whoever had authorised the payment from the church's maintenance account.

Lina sat back from the notes she'd made. What she had was all circumstantial, but it at least gave her somewhere to focus. And if what Martha Hartwood had divulged to her was correct, there was a distinct possibility that Reg Hartwood, the chairman of the church's Council of Elders, would have known about Alastair's unusual level of pastoral care visits to Grace and the dates of Heather Fountain's planned trip to Tasmania.

Her signs were pointing to Reg Hartwood as either an exploited source of information or a murderer. What she needed was solid evidence, and she needed to uncover it without spooking her suspect.

She called Thomas Holt and arranged to meet him in the morning at his mother's house, away from the prying eyes of his neighbour.

As she was getting ready to head home for the day, Lina's phone rang.

'Lina Palumbo.'

'Lina, it's Rose, Rose Travers.'

Rose sniffed loudly. Lina braced herself to hear the worst while hoping for the best.

'How is he?'

'He ... he's dead.'

'I'm so sorry, Rose.'

The room started to spin. Lina sat down.

'I gotta go. I'll talk to you later.'

The call ended. Lina pictured Rose collapsing in tears into Martin's arms, as they hung onto each other in some nondescript corridor in the bowels of the Flinders Medical Centre.

'Are you okay, Lina?'

Lina looked up into the concerned eyes of Senior Constable Nick Jordan, the twenty-five-year veteran that sat at the desk next to hers in the incident room, and took several deep breaths. 'That was Pat's daughter. He didn't make it.'

'Fuck! He didn't even look sick.'

'That was the new Pat. He was twenty kilos overweight when I first met him.' Lina shook her head. 'Still, I can't believe he's gone.'

'You going to be okay to drive home?'

'I'll be alright in a minute, Nick. I have to make some calls before I leave.'

'I'll let the desk know,' said Nick.

Lina watched him go and then tapped in DI Smith's number.

After updating DI Smith, Lina called Angela's office.

'Any news?' said Carla.

'It's not good,' said Lina. 'Is Angela there?'

'I'll put you through.'

'Lina?'

'I'm so sorry, Zia.' She took a deep breath. 'Pat didn't make it.'

'That's not what I wanted to hear. Are you okay?'

Lina was surprised by the calm tone of Angela's voice. 'Not really, but what can you do? This is the way life is.'

'What happened?'

'I don't have the details. Rose called to tell me he'd died. She wasn't up to talking about it.'

'What are you doing?'

'Getting ready to go home.'

'Come to my place. I'm going to need someone to get drunk with.'

Lina got as far as her car in the car park, the car she and Pat had travelled to Christies Beach in earlier in the day, the car they'd spent hours in together talking about all sorts of things, some of it related to their investigations. She thought of his shy smile, his gentle heart, and the words of encouragement he'd offered her whenever she'd doubted her investigative abilities.

Pat had been the first person in the force that had warmed to her and accepted her as a fellow officer. The first person not to hold a grudge because she was a woman who was good at her job. He'd been the mentor she'd needed when she'd first become a detective. She was going to miss him.

Lina rested her head in her hands on the steering wheel and sobbed, thankful she'd made it out of the station before she'd fallen apart. She let her emotions sweep through her until they subsided, and then searched through her bag until she found her tissues. She blew her nose and wiped her eyes. Then she headed into the city to pick up her own car before going to Angela's.

CHAPTER 25

REG HARTWOOD STOOD in front of his ute and watched the truck carrying the last two bins of grapes from the year's harvest make its way out of the vineyard and turn onto Chalk Hill Road.

He pushed his hat back and chewed on the piece of dry grass he'd absent-mindedly picked and put into his mouth. They'd been lucky enough to find a buyer for all of their grapes this vintage, even the Shiraz, despite the gallons of red wine sitting in storage tanks across the region waiting for the market to improve.

Although grape prices were down across all varieties, they were high enough by Reg's reckoning for them to break even. They'd just have to tighten their belts again this year. At least they hadn't had to let their grapes rot on the vine. That would have been a sacrilege he'd have found hard to live with after all the work and water that had gone into growing them.

When the truck disappeared in the direction of the winery, where his grapes were destined to be crushed and fermented, Reg climbed into his ute and drove up the track from the vineyard to the sheds behind the homestead he shared with Megan, his wife of forty years.

In the yard in front of the sheds, his son and vineyard manager, Greg, was washing down their harvester with a hose.

'Thought you were going to Maxwell's.'

'Just giving her a quick clean before I head over there. Don't want to contaminate their grapes.'

'Fair enough. I'll see you later.'

'Right, Dad.'

Reg headed towards the homestead, intent on getting himself some breakfast. He'd reached the back porch when his mobile phone rang. He glanced at the screen of his phone. It was a bit early in the day for Phil Snowdon to be calling him.

'What's got you out of bed at this ungodly hour, Phil?'

'Can't sleep. I've been arrested over that little job I did for you?'

'Have you? Where are you calling from?'

'Don't worry, I haven't said anything. I'm out on bail. Court case is months away. Anyway, we need to talk.'

'What about?' Reg thought he had a good idea of what Phil was going to say next.

'The cost of silence, Reg.'

'You got paid for your part, Phil.'

'The cops want to know who I did the job for.'

'You got paid for your silence on that.'

'Yeah, well, the price has gone up, Reg. The cops are offering me a trade. I tell them who I gave the recordings to and they'll drop the accessory to murder charge.'

'Why are they charging you with that?'

'Think about it, Reg. The people you asked me to spy on are both dead.'

'And, what? You think I killed them?'

'You asked me to install the camera and catch them at it. I gave the recordings to you. And they're dead. How do you think the cops see it?'

'That you were working for the killer.'

'Exactly! And, if I wasn't, then obviously the person I gave the recordings to had to be.'

Reg couldn't see any point in arguing with the logic of that. 'Are you considering this deal they're offering?'

'I will if you don't come to the party.'

Reg thought about the likelihood of the police believing him if he denied whatever Phil told them. They had nothing linking him to the murders. He'd made sure of that. He'd even destroyed the USB drive with the recordings on it. But what if there was something linking him to the killings he'd overlooked?

'Are you still there, Reg?'

'What figure do you have in mind?'

'What's your freedom worth to you, Reg?'

'Let's not beat about the bush, Phil. How much do you want?'

'A hundred grand, in cash.'

Reg almost laughed. Like every farmer in the country, he was asset rich and cash poor. He'd have to speak to his banker to get his hands on that much cash.

'That's a lot of money, Phil. Might take me a few days to get my hands on that much cash.'

'I'm not in any hurry, Reg. How does next Monday sound to you?'

A week. Reg shook his head. This clown had no idea

how things worked in the real world. 'Where do you want to meet for the handover?'

'Same place we used last time.'

'I'll let you know when I have the cash and we can set up a time.'

'Don't disappoint me, Reg.'

'Yeah, and don't plan on coming back for more. There won't be any.' Reg ended the call and went in for breakfast.

Reg arrived in the car park of the industrial estate opposite the Uniting Church Cemetery on Seaford Road five minutes before their agreed meeting time. He reversed parked into a bay facing the exit for a quick getaway. Before shutting off the engine, he pressed the button that sent the window down inside the driver's side door. He killed the lights and let his eyes adjust to the darkness.

Then, with his cocked, half-sized crossbow resting on the armrest of the driver's side door, he settled down to wait. A few cars went past on Seaford Road, but no-one seemed to notice him sitting alone in the dark. Five minutes later, right on time, Phil's van pulled into the car park and stopped in front of Reg's ute, blocking his exit.

Phil left his headlights on, illuminating the inside of the ute through its windscreen.

Reg turned his eyes away from the glare but made no move to get out of his vehicle. He lifted the hessian bag he'd stuffed full of cut up pieces of paper from his lap and rested it on the edge of the window frame to block Phil's view into the cabin.

Phil got out of his van and approached the ute, stopping

far enough away to be out of the range of Reg's door being forcefully opened on him.

'You got my money?'

'Want to count it?' Reg lifted the hessian bag from its perch on the driver's side door and tossed it at Phil's feet. It hit the ground with a dull thud. Phil bent and grasped the top of the bag with his right hand, momentarily taking his eyes off Reg.

Reg waited for Phil to stand up with the bag in his hand. Then, in a move he'd practised countless times, he raised the crossbow and aimed it at Phil's chest.

'What the?'

Reg squeezed the trigger, releasing the bolt. Phil dropped the bag, clutched at his chest and fell backwards onto the ground, hitting his head on the concrete edging of the car park's garden bed. Reg reloaded, got out of the ute, and walked to where Phil lay on the ground, bathed in the glow of the van's headlights.

Phil was out to it, but the rhythmic movement of his chest indicated he wasn't dead. Reg pointed the crossbow at his head and released a bolt through Phil's right eye into his brain. The rhythmic movement of Phil's chest ceased.

Reg knelt on one knee and checked for a pulse in Phil's neck. Nothing.

Reg picked up the hessian bag and threw it back into his ute. He walked across to Phil's van. Its motor was still running. He needed to move it to get out of the car park. He looked around. The headlights of a car swept past on Seaford Road. Reg got into the van and reversed it back, before driving it forward to block the view of Phil's body from the car park entrance. He switched off the lights and then the motor, then got out of the van and walked over to his ute, telling himself Phil hadn't given him any other choice.

Reg sat behind the wheel of the ute, mentally ticking off the items on his checklist to ensure he didn't leave any clues behind. Satisfied he'd covered his tracks, he slipped the crossbow back into its bag and peeled off his latex gloves. It would be hours before anyone found Phil's body.

He started the engine, switched on the headlights, and drove towards the exit onto Seaford Road, slowing as he approached the exit. There were no headlights coming in either direction. He accelerated. There was a loud bang, followed by a body in a high-vis vest sliding across the bonnet and disappearing down the side of the ute.

'Shit! Where did you come from?' Reg hit the brakes, shifted into neutral, and pulled on the handbrake.

Torn between wanting to render assistance and needing not to be there, Reg got out of the ute. There was a mangled bicycle blocking his path. He picked it up and threw it onto the nature strip. He looked up and down the road. There were no approaching headlights from either direction. He had to go.

Ignoring the moans of the fallen cyclist, Reg got back into the ute and sped off up Seaford Road towards Main South Road, planning on being back in the front bar of the Old Noarlunga before anyone had time to notice his absence.

It wasn't until he got home and examined the ute under the lights of the equipment shed, that Reg realised the impact of the collision with the cyclist had put a dent in the driver's side mudguard and shattered the glass of the turn right indicator light. And there were several deep gouges in the paintwork where the bicycle's handlebar had scraped along the side of the ute.

'Bugger!'

Reg crossed his arms and leant back against the stone wall of the shed. He'd had the ute since he'd bought it new in 2008 and managed to keep it dent free in all that time. Anybody familiar with it would notice the damage immediately and would, no doubt, tease the hell out of him. They all knew how proud he was about his old ute still looking as good as new. He'd bragged about it often enough.

He decided he'd have to arrange a minor farm related accident to disguise the true nature of the damage. Perhaps hitting the gatepost at the top of the driveway. He thought about doing it before going in but stopped himself when he realised Megan would have heard him drive in. He shook his head. It would have to wait until the morning. Besides, Megan was going up to Adelaide in the morning, and Greg would be working on things at his own place now the vintage was over.

He ran his hand over the dented mudguard and told himself waiting until morning made more sense than rushing into action in the dark. Doing it in the daylight meant he'd have a better chance of not putting the ute out of action by accident.

Decision made, he switched off the lights and headed for the house, confident Megan would leave in the morning without looking in the equipment shed. She never went in there. That was men's business. Her business was the house and all the things that made his life comfortable within it.

CHAPTER 26

Lina took Senior Constable Nick Jordan with her to interview Thomas Holt. It wasn't that she felt unsafe with the Holts. She wanted someone with her to corroborate her notes of the interview.

'Hi, Tom. This is Senior Constable Jordan.'

Thomas shook Senior Constable Jordan's hand. 'You used to be one of the local policemen, didn't you?'

'You've got a good memory, son.'

Thomas looked at Lina. 'Where's Sergeant Travers?'

'You been listening to the news?'

'No. Why?'

'He died yesterday.'

'Oh, I'm sorry to hear that. What happened?'

'Unexpected medical issue.'

'Must be tough for you, having to carry on, I mean.'

'No tougher than what it must have been for you.'

Thomas smiled and then ushered them into what had been his father's study. 'I think I've found what you're looking for. Dad kept what he called a day book. He used it to make his own notes of all church related meetings and phone calls.'

'What did you find out about the ceiling fans?'

'That one was easy. That was the Welfare Committee. There's a record of their decision to grant Grace's request for help to buy the fans at the November meeting last year.'

'Does it mention anything about paying for the installation?'

'Not in dad's notes, but I looked up the minutes.' Thomas paused. 'Did I tell you they've sacked me?'

'No. Really?'

'Yeah, I'm officially no longer the pastor.' Thomas smiled. 'But they still haven't revoked my access to the Google Drive where we store official records.'

Pretty devious for a pastor, thought Lina, impressed by his ingenuity. 'What did you find?'

'They decided to pay for the installation.'

'Who suggested that?'

'Reg Hartwood.'

'Any mention of using Snowdon Electrical?'

'Yeah. They were recommended by Henry Yates. He uses them all the time, apparently. He's a builder, oversees all our property maintenance work. Said he was happy with their work and they'd give us a good price.'

'Is there a record of the payment for the installation?'

'I don't have access to the bank accounts, but they scan in all the invoices they pay. I found one from McLaren Vale Hardware for the fans, but there's nothing from Snowdon Electrical for the installation.'

'Any record of who contacted Snowdon to arrange the installation?'

'No.'

'Well, someone must have arranged it. Sophie said Grace was told to contact him.'

'Can't you ask Phil Snowdon?'

'We've checked his records. Nothing. Claims Grace paid him cash.'

'I guess that's possible,' said Tom. 'Dad may have passed her the cash. He was one of the signatures on the Welfare Committee's account.'

'Who does the church bank with?'

'Bank SA.'

'Who else is on that committee?'

'They're all sub-committees of the Council of Elders. Reg is the chair of the Welfare Committee and Henry chairs the Property Committee.'

Control freaks, thought Lina. 'Find anything on the work Snowdon did for the church around March last year?'

'I remember that. We had him install security cameras on the church. We'd had a couple of break-ins.' Thomas smiled. 'I've made copies of everything for you.'

'Ever thought of becoming a detective?' said Lina.

'Something to think about, I suppose, if I can't find another flock looking for a shepherd.' Thomas handed the documents he'd printed to Lina.

'This will be helpful, thanks.'

'What do you think it tells you?'

'I'm not sure yet, but at least we now know who suggested Phil Snowdon be asked to install the fans.'

Lina let Nick get in behind the wheel.

'I know Henry Yates,' said Nick. 'Known him for years. Can't see him being your killer.'

'Why's that?'

'He's a good bloke. Give you the shirt off his own back.'

Lina recalled Thomas Holt remembering Nick from his time in McLaren Vale. 'How many years did you spend here before they closed the station?'

'I was here for the last six years. We almost bought a house here, but the kids didn't want to move.'

'When was the last time you saw Henry?'

'We bumped into him and Linda when we were here for lunch a couple of Sundays ago.'

'Got his number?'

'Yeah.'

'Give him a call and see if we can catch up with him before we head back.'

As she listened to Nick arrange for them to drop into the building site where Henry Yates was working, Lina was half listening to the chatter on the police radio. She stopped listening to Nick when a voice on the radio mentioned a body with two crossbow bolts wounds being found in a car park off Seaford Road.

'Did you hear that?'

'What?'

'Another body with crossbow bolts sticking out of it.'

'That can't be a coincidence.'

No, thought Lina. 'We'll need to follow that up when we get back. How did you get on with Henry?'

'He's only around the corner from here. Happy to talk to you.'

'Okay. Let's go.'

Henry Yates reminded Lina of a teddy bear. His smile was warm and genuine, his handshake firm without being crushing.

'Thank you for agreeing to talk to us, Mr Yates.'

'Please, call me Henry. How can I help?'

'You had Phil Snowdon install some security cameras at your church.'

'That's right. I use him all the time. In fact, he's supposed to be here later today.'

'I'm curious to know if you know about his sideline in covert surveillance?'

Henry looked at Nick with a sheepish smile. 'He did mention it.'

'In what context?'

'He said something about it when he was installing the security cameras. Said if I ever needed to catch someone stealing stuff from a building site or to keep an eye on me missus, he had access to some tiny, almost invisible cameras he could discreetly install for me, off the books, of course.'

'Ever use his services for those purposes?'

'Nah. I trust my work crew, and there's no way I'd want to spy on Linda. She'd kill me if she found out.'

Nick laughed. 'I wouldn't want to get on her bad side either, mate.'

'Ever mention Phil's sideline to anyone else?'

Henry's eyes went up and his smile morphed into a frown. 'You know, I think I mentioned it to the other members of the Property Committee when we were talking about the security cameras we'd installed. Yeah, I'm pretty sure I told them, only because I remember Reg saying he thought you'd need a special licence to do that sort of thing. Apparently, he'd looked it up when we were thinking about what we could do about our break-ins.'

'Anybody apart from Reg?'

'Michael, that's Michael Knolls. He owns the hardware store. Pretty sure Sam was away when we put in the security cameras. Why do you want to know?'

'Phil installed one of those cameras in Grace William's apartment when he put in her ceiling fans.'

'Why would he do that?'

'Someone asked him to, but he's not saying who.'

Henry shrugged. 'Well, I can assure you, it wasn't me.'

'Hear any talk of the relationship between Alastair and Grace before they were killed?'

'You know, I don't know how he did it right under our noses. I never suspected him for a moment, and I've been a member of the community for over thirty years. Didn't hear a whisper until after Grace was murdered.' Henry shook his head. 'Still can't believe it.'

Henry's phone rang. He looked at the screen. 'I'd better take this.'

'Thanks,' said Lina.

They had only reached the boundary of the building site when Henry called after them.

'That was Phil's lad. He's just had a visit from some of your colleagues. Phil's dead. He's been murdered.'

CHAPTER 27

DETECTIVE SERGEANT TIM HEALY and Detective Constables Kevin Snow and John Cheshire had taken up residence in the incident room by the time Lina and Nick returned from McLaren Vale.

'I see the cavalry has arrived,' said Nick. 'You going to be okay?'

'I'll be fine,' said Lina. 'I've worked with this lot before.'

'Ah, Palumbo. Wondered where you were.'

'Hello, Sergeant.'

'Sorry about Pat. How are you coping?'

'Doing my best.' Lina shrugged. 'Are you taking over as SIO?'

Tim nodded and looked at his watch. 'Briefing in ten. I'll need you to bring us up to speed and then we can go over today's incidents.'

'Incidents?'

'Let's not get ahead of ourselves, Palumbo. Grab yourself a coffee and I'll see you in ten.'

Lina headed for the kitchen to make herself a coffee, feeling relieved someone senior was taking charge but a little disappointed she hadn't been left to solve the case on her own.

Tim Healy took notes while Lina outlined her investigation and detailed the connections between Alastair Holt, Grace Williams, and Phil Snowdon.

'What I have to date points to Reg Hartwood being the person who arranged for Phil Snowdon to install the surveillance camera in Grace Williams' apartment. He knew Snowdon offered the service and was aware Holt visited her every Wednesday morning, thanks to his sister-in-law. But I've yet to confirm that and there's nothing linking him, or anybody else for that matter, to either murder.'

'Have you spoken to this Hartwood character?' said Tim.

'DS Travers interviewed him as part of our background checks on Holt but I haven't spoken to him since we found out about the covert surveillance.'

'Anything in Snowdon's records?'

'Nothing we could find, but, then again, he didn't keep anything like a full set of books.'

'Kevin, I want a full background on this Hartwood.'

'What would be his motive, Sarge?' said Kevin.

Tim turned to Lina. 'What do you think, Palumbo?'

'Hartwood and Holt were two of the foundation members of the church. Holt preached what you'd call a conservative Christian message. You know, family values, marital faithfulness, and all that sort of stuff. Think I'd be pissed off if the friend I'd trusted to guide the church we'd started together turned out to be a hypocritical liar having an affair behind my back.'

'Those scandals happen all the time,' said John.

'That might be so, but this is a small, tight-knit community. We're talking around two hundred people, including kids.'

'Okay, let's see what turns up when we put Hartwood under the microscope. Now, let me bring you up to date with today's activities.'

Lina moved away from the whiteboard and Tim took her place in front of the team.

'Uniform were called to a hit and run in front of the Uniting Church Cemetery on Seaford Road around nine forty-five last night. Cyclist collided with a white utility coming out of the car park of the industrial estate opposite the cemetery. Our cyclist, a Richard Myles, wasn't seriously hurt. Bruising and a broken collarbone. Says the driver, an older bloke, possibly in his sixties, got out, chucked his bike out of the way, and then drove off without rendering assistance. We're looking for a white Mazda utility with a broken driver's side turn indicator and possible damage to its driver's side front mudguard. Unfortunately, our Mr Myles didn't get the rego.' Tim looked at Lina. 'Now, in the normal course of events, Uniform would follow this up but, as it turns out, this doesn't exactly qualify as a normal course of events.'

'Is this where Phil Snowdon comes in?' said Lina.

'This is where that white Mazda becomes more important. We got another call-out to almost the same location at seven this morning. This time, we have a van, with Snowdon Electrical signage, and a body in the car park our white Mazda was so keen on leaving when it collided with our cyclist. The victim's been identified as Phil Snowdon. He's got a crossbow bolt firmly embedded in his chest and another one where his right eye used to be. '

'Time of death line up with the hit and run?'

'In the ballpark.'

'Black crossbow bolts?'

'You're not just a pretty face, are you, Palumbo?'

'Why don't we see what sort of vehicle Hartwood drives?' said Lina. 'Might narrow down our possibilities.'

'Something for you, John. I know how you love a good vehicle search.'

***

'Hartwood owns a white 2008 Mazda BT-50, rego number XRV 367,' said John. 'That's a ute.'

'Let's get someone out there to check it out,' said Tim.

Lina turned to Nick. 'Can you get that organised? And tell them he may be armed with a crossbow.'

'He's probably got a shotgun,' said Nick. 'Most of the landowners down here have at least one gun.'

'Let me check the register,' said John, turning back to his laptop.

They waited while he queried the gun register.

'Yeah, you're right. He's got a shotgun.'

'Okay, I'll get that organised.'

'Instruct them to say they're only checking his vehicle to eliminate him from our list of known Mazda owners, and to restrict their comments to the hit-and-run incident only. We don't want to spook him if he's our killer,' said Tim.

'I'll organise backup,' said Nick. 'We don't want them walking into trouble without backup if he's armed.'

CHAPTER 28

Reg was sitting at the kitchen table enjoying the morning tea Megan had set out for him before she'd left for the city. He wasn't expecting her back until late afternoon, by which time he'd planned to have had a little accident in his ute. He sipped his coffee and considered his options. Grazing the gatepost on the way out of the yard would probably be the least damaging method, he decided. The ute would still be drivable and, if he did it slowly enough, the gatepost would still be standing. He could claim a moment of inattention, a spider dropping from the sun visor, or some such excuse to explain it.

He finished the last of the hot scones he'd smothered in butter and apricot jam, and took his dishes to the sink. He felt his phone ringing in his pocket. As a church elder, he never went anywhere without it in case someone needed his help or advice. He slipped his hand into his pocket and pulled it out, glancing at the caller ID.

'Henry. What's up?'

'Remember Nick Jordan?'

Reg pictured the middle-aged policeman who'd been the

last officer at the local police station before it had closed and wondered why Henry had mentioned his name. 'Yeah, I remember him.'

'He's just been to see me with that lady detective, you know, the pretty one investigating Alastair's death.'

'Are you in trouble, Henry?' Reg almost laughed. He couldn't imagine Henry Yates doing anything that would get him into trouble with the police.

'No, they wanted to know if I knew anything about Phil Snowdon's surveillance sideline and whether I'd mentioned it to anybody else.'

That sounded ominous to Reg. He hadn't heard anything about the police finding the camera Phil had installed in Grace's apartment. If they knew about that, things could get tricky. 'What did you tell them?'

'That Phil had let me know he could do that sort of thing, and that I'd mentioned it to you and Michael when we were talking about the security cameras he'd installed for us.'

Reg took a slow breath and told himself to stay calm. 'Why do they want to know that?'

'They reckon Phil put one of his spy cameras up in Grace's apartment when he installed her fans.'

'Do they think Phil is some sort of pervert?'

'No, I think they're trying to find out who asked him to install it. Obviously, they found the camera, but Phil's not saying who asked him to install it. At least, that's what they told me. Who knows, you might be right. Maybe Phil's spinning them a yarn.'

'Well, we didn't ask him to do it, did we? Maybe Phil was obsessed with Grace. You know what she was like. Perhaps he killed them when he found out she was screwing Alastair after she'd brushed him off.' Reg gave himself a virtual pat on the back, telling himself that was a story that would come in handy if the police ever came looking for answers.

'Well, they're not going to get a confession out of him now.'

'What do you mean?'

'He's dead.'

Reg told himself to play a straight bat. He'd expected to hear about Phil's death, but not from Henry. 'How do you know that?'

'His son called me when the police were here. His body was found in a car park off Seaford Road first thing this morning. They're saying he was murdered.'

'That's not good, Henry. Who are you going to use for your electrical work now? Wasn't Phil your go-to man for that work?'

'His son. He's fully qualified, and he knows the work.'

'Police say anything about who they think killed Alastair?'

'No, but I don't think they had Phil down as their killer. Anyway, just thought I'd give you a heads-up in case the police come to see you.'

'Thanks, Henry. Take care, now.'

Reg ended the call and looked at his watch. It was almost eleven. He'd been putting off listening to the news all morning, but decided it might be time to find out what the police were saying about last night's hit-and-run on Seaford Road.

After the national headlines, there was a brief mention of a man's body having been discovered in a car park at Seaford, followed by an appeal for witnesses to a hit-and-run accident involving a white Mazda utility and a cyclist on Seaford Road, at around nine forty-five the previous evening. The police spokesperson announced that the Mazda, reportedly driven by an older male, possibly in his sixties, was likely damaged on the driver's side mudguard and asked for the driver to turn himself in at the nearest police station.

Damn cyclist, thought Reg. Should have put a bolt through him as well. Obviously, the bastard hadn't gotten the registration number. At least that was something. He hit the table with his fist. The sugar bowl jumped. Instinctively, he reached out to stop it from falling to the floor. He had enough things to think about, without having to contend with Megan's reaction to the destruction of one of her favourite pieces of chinaware.

As he repositioned the bowl, he wondered if his farmyard accident story would pass muster once Greg got wind of why the police were looking for a damaged ute like his. He decided he needed a plan B and realised he probably wouldn't have much time to come up with one.

Reg placed the note with its solitary word on Megan's pillow and left the house. It was too late to worry about what she'd think when the truth came out about the cyclist he'd abandoned on the side of the road. He doubted she'd forgive him for not stopping to render assistance, since the parable of the Good Samaritan was one of her favourites.

He was beyond caring what she or any of the members of the community would think about what he'd done to the others. In his mind, they'd paid the price for being caught in the act of adultery, as stipulated by the law of Moses. Phil Snowdon, on the other hand, didn't count. He was a common criminal in the service of Mammon.

From his perspective, a perspective heavily influenced

by a lifelong literal reading of scripture, Reg thought they should be thanking him for setting things right with the world and meting out God's justice, instead of talking about him as a killer. Unfortunately, despite his best efforts, Reg was all too aware they were still living in a secular world where the police enforced the laws of men and not the laws of God.

He packed an overnight bag, locked up the house, and headed into the hills, thankful he'd topped up the ute's tank on his way home from the Old Noarlunga. He didn't know where he was going or what he was going to do, but he knew he couldn't stay where he was if he was to have any say in what would happen next.

CHAPTER 29

SENIOR CONSTABLE NICK JORDAN came into the incident room and walked up to DS Tim Healy. 'There's no sign of Reg Hartwood or his ute at his place of residence, Sergeant.'

'Get them to check again later in the day. If he doesn't turn up, start asking around.'

'He's got a wife and a son,' said Nick. 'I'll get the boys to call past Greg's place. He might know where his father is.'

'Okay.'

Nick left to speak with the officers waiting in McLaren Vale for his instructions.

'Want us to track his mobile, Sarge?' said Kevin.

'Wouldn't hurt.'

Tim waited while Kevin keyed in the number.

'It's either out of range or turned off. Last ping is at eleven twenty-five this morning in McLaren Vale.'

Ten minutes later, Nick came back into the incident room. 'Greg Hartwood says he thought his father was at home today. He tried calling him while the boys were there but only got his voice mail.'

'What about the wife?'

'She's in Adelaide on her own.'

'Get an APB out on his vehicle with a warning to approach with caution.'

'Sure you're not jumping the gun, Sarge?' said Kevin.

'If Palumbo's right, Hartwood's done a runner. If she's off the mark, won't hurt to cross him off the list for the hit-and-run.'

'Yeah, I'd rather we narrowed the search instead of chasing down every Mazda owner in the district,' said John.

'Speaking of narrowing the search, John, why don't you have a chat with our cyclist about Mazda utes?'

Armed with a search warrant, Lina arrived at the Hartwood homestead with Senior Constable Nick Jordan and two uniformed constables. Megan Hartwood had called as soon as she had returned from the city and discovered Reg's terse one word note.

'What exactly are you looking for?' said Megan, when Lina handed her the search warrant in exchange for Reg's note. 'I wouldn't expect there to be any evidence of his involvement in that hit-and-run accident if his ute isn't here.'

Lina looked at the word, SORRY, that Reg had written on the sheet of pink paper in large black handwriting. The style of the handwriting reminded her of the envelope they'd found in Alastair Holt's study. 'Is this your husband's handwriting?'

'Yes. Why do you have to ask?'

Lina didn't answer that question and switched the focus of their conversation back to the search warrant. 'Where does your husband keep his shotgun?'

Megan sat down at her kitchen table. 'In the gun safe. It's on the wall in his workshop.'

'That's at the back of the big shed, isn't it?' said Nick.

'Yes,' said Megan. 'It'll be locked if the gun's in it.'

'Okay, we'll check that first,' said Nick.

'Why don't you and I have a little chat while they have a look?' said Lina. 'Can I make you a cuppa?'

Megan stood. 'No. It's my kitchen. I'll do it.'

Lina watched Megan move about the kitchen as she made them a pot of tea and found a plate of biscuits for them to nibble on while they sipped their tea.

'Do you have any idea where your husband could be?' said Lina, when Megan sat down opposite her at the table.

'He never tells me where he's going, unless it's to one of his church meetings.'

'Did he say where he was going last night?'

Megan smiled. 'Come to think of it, he did. Said he was going to the Old Noarlunga, that's a pub in Old Noarlunga, to catch up with a mate. Most times he just says he's going out and he'll be back when he gets back.'

The Hartwood's relationship sounded nothing like her parents', thought Lina. Her father wouldn't dream of not telling her mother where he was going and when he'd be home, and he wouldn't risk being late without calling her. 'Did he mention who this mate was?'

'No.'

'Mention anything about a meeting with Phil Snowdon?'

'Who's Phil Snowdon?'

'He's the electrician that installed the security cameras on your church.'

'Nothing to do with me. Reg is an elder, but I'm just an ordinary member, like everybody else.'

Lina sipped her tea and looked around the kitchen. It was almost double the size of the living room in her apartment. 'How long have you lived here, Mrs Hartwood?'

'Be twenty-two years this Christmas. We moved here after Reg's parents retired. They're in their nineties now. They live in the village in town.'

Lina recalled seeing a sign for a retirement village on her way to the farm.

'Where did you live before that?'

Megan picked up a biscuit and dunked it into her tea. 'Where our Greg lives now. We had a smaller vineyard back then and Reg worked off the farm at Lonsdale during the week until we could afford to buy the place next door.'

'Obviously not in another vineyard, then?'

'No. He was a fitter and turner, with big dreams of owning his own vineyard when we first got together. He wanted to expand so he wouldn't have to work outside the vineyard when he took over running his family's vineyard.'

That's interesting, thought Lina.

'Of course, he was still living at home then. We didn't get our own place until we were married.' Megan stared into space as if lost in a memory. 'A lot of people around here had small vineyards in those days and did what we did to make ends meet.'

'Did you work?'

'I worked in the office at the school, right up until Greg was born.'

'Is that where you met Alastair Holt? His wife told us he used to work at the school.'

Megan smiled. 'No, I got him the job there. He and Reg were as thick as thieves, right from when they were little. After high school, Alastair went off to Bible School because their families had broken away from the Anglican Church and they needed a proper pastor. He'd always talked about becoming a priest. Funny how things work out, isn't it?' She didn't wait for Lina to respond. 'Anyway, while Alastair was away, Reg did his apprenticeship and saved every cent he earned. By the time Alastair was qualified, the community had decided they needed their own church, and they bought the old Presbyterian Church property next door.'

'What did Alastair's parents do?'

'They owned the vineyard next to ours. We bought it when Alastair's father died.'

'Are you a local as well?'

'We all grew up here. Most of us stayed here. Who'd want to live anywhere else?'

'Yes, it's a lovely place,' said Lina. 'Did your husband make any use of his fitting and turning skills once you'd established yourselves on the land?'

'Reg had a side business making tools and spare parts for years. He doesn't do much of that these days, though. He still tinkers away in his workshop and sells things at the farmers' market, but I think he does that to give himself an excuse for being out of the house. Our son, Greg, does most of the work now. He's our vineyard manager.'

'Does your husband have a computer, Mrs Hartwood?'

'There's one in his office.'

'Do you use it?'

'No, I have my own laptop.'

'Does he use your laptop at all?'

'No. Why all this interest in our computers?'

'We think Phil Snowdon may have given your husband a copy of a recording he made, and he'd need access to a computer to watch it.'

'You'll have to ask him about that.'

Lina finished her tea. 'Were you aware of the relationship between Alastair and Grace Williams?'

Megan shook her head. 'Not until after Grace was murdered.'

'What did you think when Martha told you about his weekly visits to her place?'

'Didn't surprise me, really. According to Marianne, he was always out visiting people, especially those living on their own.'

'What did your husband think about it?'

Megan shrugged. 'We only ever talked about it the day Martha shared that story with us. He said it sounded like something Alastair would do.'

Lina's phone pinged. She read the text message from Nick.

'If you'd please stay here, Mrs Hartwood, I just need to attend to this.'

Lina joined Nick Jordan in the equipment shed. 'What is it?'

Nick held out his gloved hand and opened his fingers to reveal a black object they both recognised as a crossbow bolt.

'Where did you find that?'

'There's a box of them in the gun safe in the workshop through that door there.' He pointed to the back wall of the space they were standing in.

The safe had to be open, thought Lina, recalling Megan's words. 'Is there a gun in that safe?'

'No, but you can see where it's been.'

'What about a crossbow?'

'No.'

'So, he's definitely armed, then.' Lina pulled out her mobile phone and called Tim Healy.

'Looks like he's definitely armed with a shotgun and possibly with a crossbow, Sarge.'

'Getting anything from the wife?'

'Background mainly. She claims she has no idea where he'd go.'

'Speak to the son before you come back. He might have some idea where he'd be.'

Lina ended the call and turned her attention back to Nick Jordan. 'Bag up those bolts and then go in and get his computer. I doubt Mrs Hartwood will know the password but, you never know, we might get lucky.'

As Lina was walking back to the house, a white Mazda ute pulled up behind the police car parked in front of the homestead. The man that got out was too young to be Reg Hartwood, and he was accompanied by a boy of about ten in a school uniform.

'What's going on?'

'Who are you?'

'Greg Hartwood.'

'Detective Constable Palumbo.' Lina showed him her ID.

'What are you doing here?'

'Talking to your mother and conducting a search.'

'A search? I thought it was a hit-and-run accident.'

'I'm afraid it's a little more serious than that.'

'What do you mean?'

'Is this your son?' said Lina.

'Yes. This is Travis.'

'You might want to send Travis in to his grandmother. She's in the kitchen.'

'Off you go, mate. Tell Grandma I'll be there in a minute.'

They watched Travis run through the garden and disappear into the homestead.

'I think your father may have killed three people.'

Greg Hartwood stared at her. His mouth opened and closed but no words came out.

'I realise that's probably a bit of a shock coming out of the blue like that.'

'You can say that again.'

'Do you use the workshop at the back of that shed?' Lina pointed to the equipment shed.

'No, that's Dad's play space. That's where he makes things to sell at farmers' markets.'

'Is that where he stores his shotgun?'

'Yeah, there's a gun safe on the back wall.'

Lina crossed her arms. 'The safe's empty.'

'That's not good.'

'Does your father have a crossbow?'

'A crossbow? Not that I know of.'

'I think he does,' said Lina. 'We found a box of crossbow bolts inside his gun safe.'

Greg frowned. 'How do you know they're crossbow bolts?'

'We have three bodies with bolts like the ones we found in your father's safe embedded in them.'

'Bloody hell!' Greg leant back on the front of his ute.

'Any idea where your father may have gone? Places he goes to chill out?'

'If he's gone anywhere, he's probably gone fishing down

the Coorong. That's what he does when he needs to think things through.'

'Is there any way we could tell?'

'His fishing rods. They'd be gone.'

'Where does he keep them?'

'In that shed, where he usually parks his ute.'

'Let's check, shall we?'

Lina followed Greg into the equipment shed and looked up to where he pointed at a bundle of fishing rods firmly attached to the rafters.

'I don't know where he'd be if he hasn't gone fishing.'

'He might still have gone down there,' said Lina. 'Where precisely does he go?'

'We usually camp on 90 Mile Beach, near 42 Mile Crossing.'

CHAPTER 30

ALTHOUGH PAT HAD DIED on duty, he hadn't died in the line of duty. This distinction meant his funeral service was a family affair and not a state sponsored police funeral with extensive media coverage.

His children had chosen St Ignatius Catholic Church, Norwood, for the service. St Ignatius had been the family's parish church until their mother died, after which Pat had sold the family home on Beulah Road and moved across the city to Glenelg.

Lina sat next to Angela on a pew between the family and the considerable police contingent in attendance, among which sat the Commissioner, who had been in Pat's class at the Police Academy. As they'd walked in, Lina had spotted DCI Max Roberts sitting next to the Commissioner. Max Roberts had been to Pat what he'd been to her.

In the front pew, she could see Rose supporting her grandmother, a frail-looking woman who had entered the church through a side door with the assistance of a walking frame. Sitting alongside Pat's son, Alex, in his air force blue was a young woman in a naval uniform, who Lina presumed was the Felicity she'd heard so much about. Pat had been so proud of his children and their partners. He hadn't stopped talking about them in the nearly three years she'd worked with him.

She shook her head. Had it only been that long? It had seemed like a lot longer when she'd first tried to take stock after his death. She squeezed Angela's hand.

'How are you doing, Zia?'

Angela squeezed her hand back without speaking.

Lina knew Angela had cried herself out, and not for the first time. Giorgio, her husband of eighteen years, had been knocked off his bike and killed on Portrush Road, almost within spitting distance from where they were sitting. Life definitely isn't fair, thought Lina.

She looked around. There were a number of people she didn't recognise. She assumed they were friends and associates from Pat's life outside the force.

The priest finished splashing holy water over the coffin and turned to read the opening prayer.

Lina had been to a few funerals in her time, but Pat's was the first she'd been to for a colleague. Most of the others had been for elderly relatives or friends of the family.

Rose had compiled a collection of photographs of the highlights of Pat's life, which were screened after the eulogies. It was the first time Lina had seen pictures of Pat's wife, Pam, who'd died five years before she'd met Pat. Lina could see echoes of Pam in Rose, while she thought Alex looked a lot like his father had when he'd been younger.

In Lina's opinion, Alex did a good job of telling stories

about his father, some of which elicited laughter from the congregation. The Commissioner spoke on behalf of the force and as a friend. Lina learnt a few things about Pat's service in the years before she'd met him that he hadn't mentioned in their many conversations.

She knew he was regarded as a highly respected investigator. Everyone around her had told her that. But she'd had no idea he'd been awarded a medal for bravery during his time as a uniformed constable on the beat in Pt Adelaide, when he'd risked his life jumping into the Port River fully clothed to rescue a toddler who'd fallen into the water. Perhaps she hadn't heard about it before because the episode had occurred when she was a five-year-old but, it was more likely, she decided, she hadn't heard about it because of Pat's modesty. He'd always talked up other people, including her, and had never bragged about his own achievements in her hearing, apart from going on about his kids.

When the service ended, Lina drove Angela to Centennial Park, where Pat was interred in the same grave as Pam. Rose explained it was what they'd agreed when Pam was dying. She'd been the love of his life, right from the day they'd met at high school, and they'd wanted to be buried together forever.

Angela said she understood. She was planning on being buried in the same plot as Giorgio in another corner of Centennial Park, not too distant from where they stood.

After the interment, they visited Giorgio's grave and then joined Pat's family for lunch at the Edinburgh in Mitcham, where Lina heard more stories about the Pat she had hardly known, and told a few stories of her own about the man she'd worked with and admired.

CHAPTER 31

REG HARTWOOD, Alastair Holt, Michael Knolls, Henry Yates and Sam Westwood became fast friends during their first year at school together as boisterous boys. Reg was the only first-born and, being accustomed to bossing around a younger brother, was soon asserting his will on his mates, directing their play and deciding what and when they'd do things. It wasn't long before everyone was calling them 'the five', since they did everything together.

As they grew older, they threw themselves into sport and mischief making, although their mischief making was some-what constrained by the conservative religious values of their upbringing. Besides going to school together during the week, the boys attended the same Sunday School every Sunday at the local Anglican Church, where their parents were the core members of the conservative part of the congregation.

During their adolescent years, the boys competed for the attention of the same group of girls, played on the same sporting teams, and were active members of the youth group run by the local Anglican priest. Despite their common interests, however, by the time they reached the senior years of high school, they found themselves on divergent academic and career pathways.

Although the boys all came from vineyard owning families, those vineyards were not financially successful enough to support more than one son working with his father. Reg, as a first-born son, was destined to take over his family's vineyard. His career path had been mapped out for him at birth, although he had to branch out and find an off-farm income in the early days due to the fluctuating nature of the prices growers received for their grapes.

However, as second sons, the others had to find alternative pathways for life. Sam, who wanted to work in the wine industry, set his sights on becoming a winemaker. Henry took an apprenticeship with a local builder. Michael, who was already working in the local hardware store part-time, decided he'd become an accountant. Alastair, the most studious of the five, thought he'd been called to become an Anglican priest.

Only Alastair's path didn't go as planned. He ended up going to Bible College instead of the Anglican Seminary when the families of the five became embroiled in the protests against the ordination of women in the Anglican Church.

Led by Reg's father, the conservative core of the Anglican congregation they'd belonged to all their lives, decided to form their own community church and despatched Alastair to Bible College so they'd eventually have a formally trained pastor.

Initially, the Southern Vales Community Church convened in the homes of its members, with the male head of each hosting family leading the service but, as the group grew in size, that arrangement became unworkable. By the time Alastair had completed his studies and was qualified to lead the Church as its pastor, the founding families had pooled their funds and purchased the vacant Presbyterian church and manse located on Chalk Hill Road on the edge of McLaren Vale, conveniently adjacent to Hartwood's vineyard.

The Church prospered under Alastair's leadership. He was a gifted preacher and appeared to live out the values he preached. He worked either on the family farm or in the local community until the Church could afford to pay him a living wage. The Elders who had overseen the development of the Church were happy to step back from preaching and pastoral care duties, but they kept a firm grip on the Church's finances and the evangelical tone of Alastair's preaching.

After serving the Community for five years, Alastair married Marianne, one of the daughters of founding members James and Helen Cole. Two years later, they had a son, Thomas.

Despite their different callings, the five continued to be best mates. Over time, they became the Church Elders as their parents withdrew into retirement and the cohesion they had enjoyed since childhood helped them build a vibrant Church with a consistent message.

When he was in his forties, Alastair's faith was tested when his father and older brother died of heart failure within a month of each other. But, as far as anyone could tell, despite his private misgivings and doubts, Alastair held firm. He'd continued to preach the same message of placing your trust in God and following his commandments. People admired him for his commitment and his example.

The sale of the Holt family vineyard after the death of Alastair's brother not only allowed Reg Hartwood to expand his operation, it also provided Alastair with the cash to purchase the house in Galaxy Court and to fund the commitment he'd eventually make to Grace Williams after the birth of Sophie.

The social lives of the five revolved around each other. Not only were they the best of mates, they were the focal point of the social life of the Church Community. To anyone looking in from the outside, they were living stable, conservative lives in line with their values. For over forty years, there had been no divorces and no scandals. The five had been rock solid in their support for each other and the values they lived.

No-one had looked beyond the facades - until Reg heard about Alastair's regular visits to Grace Williams.

Grace was a member of the Church and had turned to Alastair for support when her husband had died shortly after their wedding. When, several years later, she'd become a single mother out of wedlock, the Church Community had supported her despite her obvious failure to live up to her professed values. Alastair had preached forgiveness, using Jesus' response in the story about the woman caught in adultery. But Sophie was now fifteen and a member of the Community along with her mother. Why Alastair was still visiting her every Wednesday morning was a mystery to Reg, and it niggled at him every time he saw her with Alastair.

Grace was a bit of a stunner. Truth be told, Reg would have liked to have bedded her himself except for that bothersome commandment: thou shalt not commit adultery! He'd wanted to dismiss the story as gossip. He'd entrusted the direction of his spiritual life to Alastair's preaching and couldn't bring himself to believe that Alastair would ever do such a thing. But the whispers wouldn't go away.

Then, not long after he'd heard the story, Alastair presented Grace's request to the Welfare Committee for financial assistance to replace her ceiling fans, and Reg succumbed to the temptation to find out if the implications of the story were true or not, especially after Henry recommended they get Phil Snowdon to install the fans. Reg took that coincidence as a sign from God.

The waiting had been almost unbearable and when Phil had given him the recordings, confirming his suspicions, Reg had been incensed. He'd wanted to tell the others, but to do that he'd have had to confess to asking Phil to install the hidden camera. It would also have meant exposing Alastair as a fraud and risk destroying the Community. Reg didn't want that. He liked things the way they were.

In the end, he decided to act as God's avenger and dispense His justice in secret.

Reg hated indecision. He liked to decide and then proceed to action, but he couldn't decide what he wanted to do. Did he want to surrender to the police or take his chances with God? He'd have to choose one way forward. He knew he couldn't run forever and he couldn't stay where he was. His dilemma was in deciding which option would deliver the better outcome in the eyes of God.

He glanced at the shotgun resting in the footwell in front of the passenger's seat, then turned away to look at the ocean.

He was used to being in control, being the one who

called the shots. It had been that way as far back as he could remember.

He'd been the leader of the five almost from the day they'd started school together, sixty years ago. Thinking of the boys they'd been back then brought a smile to his face. Blond-haired, blue-eyed little devils with smiles that would melt any mother's heart. Pictures of innocence that made him think of his grandson, Travis. What would he think about his grandfather when the truth came out?

If he turned himself in, he'd get at least twenty-five years. Would Travis come to visit him in prison? Probably not. He doubted Greg would ever forgive him, even if Megan did after he'd explained it to her. At least, he hoped she'd forgive him. Maybe she wouldn't. Could he live with that?

He looked at the gun again. Might be best to end it and not have to worry about how those he loved would react. But, and it was a big but, would God see it the way he had?

He hadn't committed adultery but, in administering God's justice, he had killed three people, even though one of them hadn't been caught in the act of adultery. Would God reward him for following the law of Moses or condemn him to hell for taking the law into his own hands? At least, if he surrendered to the police, he'd get an opportunity to ask God for His forgiveness and serve his sentence on earth and not in hell. Twenty-five years sounded like a long time, but it was insignificant when compared to eternity.

He looked into the rear-view mirror. The crinkled eyes of a man who'd spent a lifetime working in the sun stared back at him. He took off his hat and scratched his head. His youthful blond hair was almost entirely gone, the remaining strands stark white and thin to the touch.

They were all turning sixty-five this year. He had

already celebrated, as had Alastair, but unlike the rest of them, Alastair wouldn't be getting any older. Henry would be celebrating his sixty-fifth birthday next month. The invitation to his party was stuck on the door of the fridge in their kitchen with one of Megan's butterfly magnets. Sam and Michael would celebrate the month after Henry. Reg didn't think any of them would want him to attend now, even if he handed himself in. Too bad, he liked a good party.

He wondered if they'd let him out on bail or insist on keeping him in the Remand Centre until he went on trial. Would Megan visit him? He knew Greg wouldn't. He'd be as disappointed in him as he had been in Alastair when he'd learnt the truth. At least Greg wouldn't be foolish enough to take the law into his own hands and test the patience of God like he had. He was a sensible son and one Reg was proud of. He knew more about growing grapes and managing a vineyard than Reg had at his age. No matter what happened, he knew their business would be in capable hands and that Greg would look after his mother.

He thought of another option. He could admit to the hit-and-run and deny the murders. They'd have a hard time pinning them on him, especially since he'd tossed the crossbow and his spare bolts into the ocean and taken precautions against leaving any evidence behind him when he'd used it. Besides, no-one even knew he'd ever had a crossbow. Could be fun seeing if they could pin the murders on him and, if luck or God were on his side, he might only get a few years instead of the twenty-five the courts so often imposed. Might be worth a try, if his conscience would let him play that hand instead of confessing to everything up front.

His thoughts drifted to Thomas and he wondered if

they'd made the right decision about forcing him out. The younger members of the Community liked Thomas. Reg had always thought of Thomas as a younger version of Alastair because he resembled the Alastair of his youth but, on reflection, he realised Thomas was nothing like Alastair as a person. For a start, he had a heart and believed in the Gospel message he preached. Another mistake he could only hope to address if he went back to face the music.

Thinking of Thomas made him think about Marianne. He'd never understood why she'd married Alastair. She just wasn't his type. After their wedding she'd slowly transformed from a vibrant young woman into a docile pastor's wife, who'd taken St Paul's direction for wives to submit to their husbands way too literally. Then again, Alastair had often preached on that very passage. Perhaps that was why his father's friends had been so keen on young Alastair's preaching.

When he'd raised the issue with Megan, after one of Alastair's frequent sermons on the topic, she'd told him where he could shove that idea if he wanted to stay married to her. As a dutiful wife, Megan gave him deference but not servitude. He respected her for that. But Marianne had given Alastair both for thirty-five years, and the duplicitous bastard had repaid her loyalty with adultery.

Reg wanted to punch Alastair's lights out all over again and wished he'd made the bastard suffer in retribution, instead of executing him as soon as he'd opened the door. As God's avenger, he'd acted in silence. But in hindsight, he wondered if he'd acted with too much haste. None of his victims had suffered, not even Phil, who'd knocked himself out cold before Reg had fired the second bolt that silenced him.

Maybe God would look favourably on his level of mercy and restraint. At least, he consoled himself, he wasn't a monster who had taken delight in making his victims suffer.

Reg got out of the car and set up a basic campsite. He'd decide what to do in the morning. For now, he'd enjoy something to eat and a night sleeping under the stars. He opened a can of spaghetti in tomato sauce and meatballs and leant back against the side of the Mazda. He sat without thinking, watching the sun sink below the horizon, taking no notice of the display of colours painting the sky in shades of pink and orange before fading into blackness. He used a fork to eat the cold spaghetti. The taste made him think about the first time he'd gone fishing with his father on this very beach, on a night when they hadn't caught a thing.

A couple of lights appeared on the beach in the distance. Headlights. Probably a couple of locals planning a spot of night fishing from the beach, thought Reg, as he eased himself up from the sand and watched the glowing orbs jiggle around and gradually grow brighter as the vehicles behind them approached his campsite.

The lead vehicle was less than a hundred metres away when the night erupted with a roaring noise that swept in off the ocean, drowning out the sound of the waves hitting the shoreline. A bright light came out of the sky and blinded him. Flying sand stung the exposed parts of his body. Reg instinctively dropped to his knees, closed his eyes, and covered his face with his hands.

The noise abated and sand stopped cutting into him as the helicopter rose into the night sky above his campsite. When he opened his eyes, he was looking into the barrel of a service revolver in the hands of a man clad in black.

'Police! Put your hands on your head! Stay where you are!'

As he sat in the rear of the police vehicle, staring at the back of the head of the driver taking him back to Adelaide, Reg decided he'd admit to the hit-and-run accident. After all, they had his damaged ute, and the cyclist had apparently seen enough of his face to identify him. And he realised, in his haste, he'd handled the guy's bike with his bare hands, so they probably had his prints as well.

May as well admit his mistake. At least the guy hadn't been seriously hurt. He might even get off with a good behaviour bond if he expressed enough remorse, although he'd have to live with the shame of not being a Good Samaritan. He couldn't see that going down well in the church community. No doubt, even if he escaped a prison sentence, he'd have to resign from his position on the Council of Elders.

As to anything else, he wasn't admitting a thing. He was sure he'd covered his tracks and left no evidence behind they could use to incriminate him. God was on his side. He wasn't the one who'd committed adultery. They'd just have to keep looking for someone else to blame for their murders. He hoped God wouldn't hang him out to dry for choosing to silence Phil Snowdon.

He wondered why the second police vehicle had stayed at his campsite and why they simply hadn't driven his ute back in convoy. Perhaps they wanted to look over his campsite in daylight, he thought, not that they'd find anything, apart from his swag and the cache of provisions he'd taken to tide him over while he decided what to do.

They already had his shotgun, and he no longer needed those provisions. He'd decided what he was going to do. All he had to do now was live with the consequences.

As the patrol car sped towards their destination, Reg stopped staring at the back of the driver and gazed out into the passing darkness, and hoped he'd made the right choice.

CHAPTER 32

WHILE UNIFORM CONVERGED on 90 Mile Beach after reported sightings of Reg Hartwood's Mazda heading south from Meningie had come in, Lina focused on finding something to connect Reg to Phil Snowdon's murder. She had her suspicions and a working hypothesis, but needed to explain why Reg had been in the car park where Phil's body had been found, and evidence showing they had been there at the same time.

Without that evidence, a lawyer could argue the hit-and-run Reg was involved in as he was leaving the car park was not connected to Snowdon's death, despite the pathologist's estimate of Phil's time of death being around the time of Reg's exit from the car park. A good lawyer would claim coincidence.

The only potential link was the crossbow bolts, but the ones embedded in Phil's body were clean in a forensic sense, even though the bolts recovered from Reg's workshop were covered in his prints.

Besides, although Ballistics had told her they could show the bolts had been manufactured by the same machine, they'd also told her she had a problem. They couldn't prove the bolts retrieved from the victims' bodies had been fired from the same crossbow, even if they had the crossbow. And the reason, they'd explained, was simple. A crossbow is a smooth-bore weapon, without rifling and a firing pin, and leaves no identifying marks on bolts fired from it.

Lina put the bolts aside and reviewed Phil's phone records for the period between when he'd been released on bail and the night he'd been killed. There were several calls to Henry Yates and his mobile phone's location data revealed he'd visited McLaren Vale on three occasions. A quick conversation with Henry confirmed Phil and his son had been on site doing electrical work on the house he was building in McLaren Vale on those dates.

After speaking to Henry, she spotted Reg Hartwood's number on Phil's outgoing calls log. It was the first call Phil had made on the Monday morning a week prior to his death. As she ran her eyes down the screen, she noticed it was also the last number Phil had received a call from on the day he'd been murdered. Apart from being calls she'd have to ask Reg about when they found him, the record of their existence was a clear sign of a connection between the two.

Unfortunately for Lina, Reg's phone records revealed he had switched off his mobile on the night Phil Snowdon had been killed. While she was lamenting her lack of luck, her laptop pinged, announcing the arrival of an email.

She looked at the notification. The sender was from Crime Scene Investigations. She opened the email. It contained a brief message describing a video file retrieved from Reg Hartwood's computer and a link to a copy of the file stored on their ShareDrive. Apparently Reg had deleted several files in early February, weeks before Alastair Holt's murder, but failed to empty the Recycle Bin on his computer.

Lina clicked on the link and played the video. It didn't take her long to identify the setting. It was an overhead shot of Grace William's bedroom, and she'd seen the bodies of the two people featured in the recording before.

Lina smiled. She had the definite link between Phil Snowdon and Reg Hartwood she'd been looking for. Even if they couldn't find evidence placing Reg at any of the murder scenes, she had proof he knew about the surveillance and the affair between Alastair and Grace prior to their deaths.

Maybe, she thought, it was something that wasn't there that she needed to find. She checked the location data for Reg's mobile on the night Alastair Holt had been killed. It had not pinged any towers between seven and ten twenty that night. She scrolled to the date for the morning Grace Williams had been shot. Reg's mobile had been off air that morning between eight and eleven fifteen. Interesting, thought Lina. Every other day he'd kept his phone on all day and all night.

She wondered how he'd respond when questioned, and if they'd get the opportunity to interview him. Reg wouldn't be the first person to shoot himself instead of facing the humiliation of being tried for murder, and she hoped he wouldn't take that path. People like Sophie and Marianne deserved answers, and they wouldn't get them if Reg took what Lina saw as the cowards' way out.

Lina was at home making herself dinner when Tim Healy called.

'We've picked up Hartwood. He was camped on 90 Mile Beach.'

'Yes, got him!' Lina said to herself, air punching with her free arm. 'How long before we can talk to him?'

'A couple of hours, at least. It's a bit of a drive from down there.'

Lina glanced at the clock on her kitchen wall. It was just after eight. 'When do you want me to come in?'

'I've arranged for his lawyer to meet us at the Watch House at ten. Probably best if we meet at nine to go over what you have.'

'Sure. Did they say anything about a crossbow?'

'Nah. He only had the shotgun with him, but CSI will go over his vehicle and campsite in the morning.'

'Okay, see you there.'

Lina returned her attention to her cooking, thinking it would be nice to have someone to share it with, someone she could talk to about things other than the case she was working on. She was envious of people like Tim, who had partners to go home to at the end of each day.

She had had little luck with finding a long-term partner. Most of the men she'd dated wanted the benefits of a relationship without wanting to make a commitment, and the others couldn't cope with her being a police officer. She doubted she could cope with her partner being in the job as well, which was why she'd kept her work relationships professional.

She thought of Thomas Holt and wondered what it would be like sharing her life with someone like him. Then she pushed that thought aside and wolfed down her meal. She was due at the Watch House with her evidence by nine, and it would take her thirty minutes to drive there at this time of night.

———

While Lina was driving into the city, a bored senior constable and his patrol partner were discussing the current state of the world and stretching their legs in the moonlight, on the expanse of wet sand that had been exposed by the receding tide in front of Reg Hartwood's campsite on 90 Mile Beach.

The senior constable stopped walking. 'What's that?'

'Where?'

'There.' The senior constable pulled his torch from his utility belt, flicked on its light, and pointed it at the dark object in the sand.

'Looks like that crossbow they asked us to look for.'

'Here, hold this!' The senior constable passed his torch to his partner and took out his phone. 'Shine the light on it!' He snapped several shots of the black object at their feet and then checked to confirm he had a clear image. Satisfied, he slipped his phone back into his pocket, pulled out a pair of latex gloves from his utility belt, and picked up the crossbow. It was heavier than he had anticipated, but not so heavy that he couldn't carry it with one hand.

'Looks like our mate forgot the tide goes out.'

'Probably wasn't expecting anyone to come down this way for a few days. It wouldn't take long for something this heavy to bury itself in the sand.'

CHAPTER 33

REG HARTWOOD SAT in silence next to the young man his law firm had sent to represent him and watched as Lina followed Tim into the interview room. His clothing was dishevelled, his hair resembled a white bird's nest, and his face was adorned with a fuzz of white stubble. Lina knew he'd been offered something to eat and drink when he'd been booked into the Watch House, but going by his appearance thought he looked at the point of collapse.

Lina activated the recording device. Tim walked them through the formalities and then asked his first question.

'Can you confirm for the record, Mr Hartwood, that you are the owner of a white Mazda utility with the registration number XRV 367?'

Reg looked at his lawyer, who nodded.

'Yes.'

'And this is the vehicle you were with when you were arrested earlier this evening?'

'Yes.'

'Can you tell us where this vehicle was on Monday night between nine and ten pm?'

Reg looked at his lawyer.

'My client admits to the hit-and-run on Seaford Road that night,' said the lawyer.

'Why didn't you stop and render assistance, Mr Hartwood?'

Reg shrugged. 'I know I should have, but I didn't.'

'Fortunately, the cyclist you hit was not seriously injured, but you will be charged with reckless driving, failing to render assistance, and leaving the scene of an accident.'

'I understand that,' said Reg. 'I'm sorry.' He leant forward and looked directly at Tim. 'Will I have to go to prison?'

'That will be up to the Magistrate,' said Tim.

Reg collapsed back into his seat.

'As you're probably aware, Mr Hartwood, the body of Phil Snowdon was found in the car park you were driving out of on Monday night when you collided with that cyclist. Know anything about that?'

'Only what I heard on the radio.'

'Let me remind you, Mr Hartwood, this interview is being recorded, and it will not be in your best interest if it turns out you're not being honest with us.'

Reg looked at his lawyer.

'You don't have to answer any of their questions, Mr Hartwood, if you don't want to. You don't have to tell them anything. If they want to charge you with something, they need to prove it.'

'I don't want to answer any more questions,' said Reg.

'That's your prerogative,' said Tim, 'but that won't stop us from asking them.'

Reg shrugged. 'Suit yourself.'

'There are a couple of interesting things about Phil

Snowdon's death I want to bring to your attention. The pathologist has determined his time of death to be around the time you were exiting the car park, and that his death was caused by someone firing a crossbow bolt into his head through his right eye and another one into his chest.'

Tim opened his folder and slid out a photograph of a black crossbow bolt. 'Ever seen one of these, Mr Hartwood?'

Reg crossed his arms over his chest. 'No comment.'

'For the record, I have just shown Mr Hartwood a photograph of a crossbow bolt retrieved from the body of Phil Snowdon.' Tim slid a second photograph out of his folder and placed it next to the first on the table in front of Reg and his lawyer.

Reg looked at the photograph and jutted out his chin.

Interesting response, thought Lina, making a note on her pad.

'This is a photograph of crossbow bolts found in your gun cabinet, Mr Hartwood. As far as our ballistics people can tell, these bolts and the ones used to kill Phil Snowdon, Alastair Holt, and Grace Williams appear to have been made using the same machinery. Mind telling us where you got the ones found in your gun cabinet from?'

'No comment.' Reg turned to his lawyer. 'They're trying to stitch me up.'

'They're showing us what they think they know, Mr Hartwood. Isn't that right, Sergeant?'

'Yes. We're trying to work out if you had the means to commit any of these murders and if you had a motive. I think we have already established that you had, at the very least, an opportunity to confront Phil Snowdon on the night he died.'

'That doesn't mean they can prove you did,' said the lawyer.

'But, we have come across a few things I'd like you to explain,' said Tim, 'which I'll get DC Palumbo to go through with you.'

Lina heard the ping announcing an incoming message on Tim's phone as she opened her folder. She waited while he glanced at his phone before slipping it back into his pocket. She slid a document out of her folder. 'This is a copy of the statement Phil Snowdon gave us, in which he admits to secretly installing a surveillance camera in Grace Williams' apartment when he installed her ceiling fans. He also told us he gave the recordings he made of Grace Williams and Alastair Holt using that camera to the person who had asked him to install it. He wouldn't tell us who that person was. Professional confidentially and all that was how he put it, but I think you know who that person is, Mr Hartwood, don't you?'

'What? How the hell would I know?'

'Steady, Mr Hartwood,' said the lawyer. 'You don't have to answer beyond saying no comment.'

Reg glared at Lina and then lowered his eyes to the tabletop.

'While you were doing whatever it was you did down the Coorong, Mr Hartwood, we conducted a search of your property. That's how we uncovered those bolts, and it's how we retrieved this video file from your computer.' Lina opened her laptop, activated the video player, and turned the laptop around so Reg and his lawyer could view the video file she had opened, and watched the colour drain from Reg's face.

'This shows my client knew about the recording,' said the lawyer. 'It doesn't mean he asked for it to be made or that he killed anybody.'

'There are a few other dots, as my former sergeant would have said, I'm afraid,' said Lina, 'otherwise we wouldn't have been able to persuade the magistrate to issue a search warrant.'

'Like what?' said the lawyer.

'There were a couple of phone conversations between your client and Phil Snowdon in the week before Phil was murdered. One on the Monday a week before and one on the day. The first was instigated by Phil, but the second was made by Mr Hartwood to Phil.'

'How much did he want, Reg?' said Tim.

'A hundred... Shit!' Reg put his head in his hands.

'Why did he want the money?' said Lina.

Reg looked at his lawyer and shook his head. 'To keep quiet about giving me the recording.'

'What did you want the recording for?'

'What does it matter? Somebody killed Alastair before I could confront him about his adultery.'

Good recovery, thought Lina, but I haven't told you everything we know yet.

'Are you sure that somebody wasn't you?' said Tim.

CHAPTER 34

REG HAD GONE into the interview prepared to admit to the hit-and-run accident. He knew not stopping had been a mistake, but he'd panicked; not that he'd told his lawyer about that and why.

After listening to his story, his lawyer had explained that, given his age, his lack of a criminal record and his expressions of remorse, he'd definitely lose his licence but probably get off with a suspended sentence. Reg thought he could live with that. His real punishment would be living with the shame of not living up to Megan's lofty standards and the expectations of the Community, and having to resign from the Council of Elders in disgrace.

The part of the interview dealing with the hit-and-run had gone quickly, but now they were questioning him about Phil Snowdon. He'd expected they'd think there was a connection between two events which had occurred in the same place at roughly the same time, but he was confident he had covered his tracks. Then DS Healy showed him the photographs of the crossbow bolts.

His lawyer had advised him to answer with 'no

comment' whenever the police asked a question designed to get information from him that had nothing to do with the accident, and explained their strategy for the interview was getting a clear idea of what the police thought they knew about whatever it was they suspected he had done.

That had all sounded reasonable before the police started revealing their evidence and letting him know they'd searched his farm. That pissed him off. They'd done that behind his back. He struggled to repress the outrage he felt at their intrusion into his home.

Looking at the photograph of the crossbow bolts next to a box that had once held shotgun cartridges, a box he recognised, Reg was no longer confident he'd been as careful as he'd told himself he'd been.

He almost laughed when DS Healy asked him where he'd gotten the bolts from, thinking the clown wasn't smart enough to realise he'd made the bloody things and couldn't resist the urge to claim they were trying to frame him. Fortunately, his lawyer stepped in and reminded him of their strategy, which got him back on track.

Reg didn't think much of female police officers at the best of times and had assumed DC Palumbo was attending the interview as a kind of official witness. He was annoyed when DS Healy turned the interview over to her and nearly lost it when she implied he knew who Phil had given the recording to, but was saved again by the quick intervention of his lawyer.

When she showed them the video he thought he had deleted from his computer, he was so flabbergasted he didn't even hear what his lawyer said about it. What he wanted to know was how they got hold of it, if he'd deleted it. But he couldn't very well ask them, could he?

Then she was rabbiting on about phone calls and, caught off guard by DS Healy's question, he blurted out an answer before realising what he was saying. Realising they'd tricked him, he knew he'd have to come up with something to take the spotlight from him. Then the answer popped into his head.

'Why did he want the money?' said DC Palumbo

Reg looked at his lawyer and shook his head to tell him he had it under control. 'To keep quiet about giving me the recording.'

'What did you want the recording for?'

'What does it matter? Somebody killed Alastair before I could confront him about his adultery.'

That should send them down a rabbit hole, thought Reg, giving himself a virtual pat on the back.

'Are you sure that somebody wasn't you?' said DS Healy.

'Are you accusing my client of a crime, DS Healy?'

'Where were you on the night Alastair Holt was killed?' said DC Palumbo, as if it was the next logical question.

'I've already answered that question. Told that Travers chap I was home with my wife!'

DC Palumbo adjusted her notes. He'd underestimated her. She was dangerous. He'd have to be careful how he answered any of her questions.

'Mr Hartwood, are you aware a mobile phone continually broadcasts its location to the mobile network and enables us to track its location over time?'

Where the hell is she going with this? 'No comment.'

'We've looked at the location data of your mobile phone for the last six months. It spends most of its time in and around your home at McLaren Vale and, from what I can tell, it's on twenty-four-seven. Is that right?'

Funny question, thought Reg. Where else would it be? 'I'm a church elder. People want to talk to me at all hours.'

'So, you take it with you wherever you go, just in case someone wants to call you?'

Reg nodded. 'Doesn't everybody?'

'I'll take that as a yes,' said DC Palumbo.

'Where are we going with this?' said the lawyer.

'To an anomaly,' said DC Palumbo, sliding several sheets of paper out of her folder. 'Each of these sheets is a printout of the location data for Mr Hartwood's mobile phone. This one,' she slid the page towards him, 'is for the Thursday night Alastair Holt was killed. This one,' she slid a second sheet across the table, 'is for the Wednesday morning Grace Williams was killed, and this one,' she slid the third sheet across the table, 'is for the Monday night Phil Snowdon was killed.'

'Why are we looking at them?' asked the lawyer.

DC Palumbo tapped the first sheet with her pen. 'Alastair Holt was killed between eight and eleven pm. This data shows Mr Hartwood's phone was not communicating its location to the network between seven and ten twenty that night.'

Shit, thought Reg. He could see where this was going.

'That would mean it was either turned off or had a flat battery, wouldn't it?' said the lawyer.

'Yes,' said DC Palumbo, tapping the three pages in turn. 'What we have here is a pattern. We have three murder victims, all killed in the same way, and all connected to the recording of an adulterous affair in the possession of your client.'

'Where's the pattern?' said the lawyer.

'Every time one of our victims was killed, your client's

mobile phone was switched off, and despite his no comment earlier, I'm sure he knows about mobile phone location data since he switched his phone off earlier today when he fled McLaren Vale. How do you explain this pattern, Mr Hartwood?'

'No comment.'

'That's all circumstantial,' said the lawyer. 'You have nothing placing my client at any of the locations where these crimes took place, apart from being in the vicinity of the car park where Phil Snowdon was murdered. And where's your murder weapon? All you've got is those dart thingies you claim you found in his gun safe.'

'Do you own or have you ever owned a crossbow, Mr Hartwood?' said DS Healy.

Reg thought of the crossbow he'd never intended to use as a weapon. He'd made it as a personal challenge to pass the time when there was nothing worth watching on TV of a night. It had taken him months to perfect the design and master its use. It was a beautiful piece of kit. He pictured the flight of the bolts he'd fired into the ocean as he'd stood on 90 Mile Beach that afternoon, before he'd walked to the water's edge and flung the crossbow into the water. He could see it arcing.above the waves and disappearing with a tiny splash. 'No comment.'

DS Healy pulled his phone out of his pocket and opened the Messages app. 'There are a couple of constables down on 90 Mile Beach securing your vehicle and campsite, Mr Hartwood. They sent this through just as we were getting under way. Care to tell me how this ended up in the sand in front of your campsite on a remote beach?'

Reg looked at the photo and wanted to slide under the table into oblivion.

'Mr Hartwood?'

'No comment.'

'This is either your crossbow or a crossbow belonging to someone you know that you dumped earlier today. If it had been there any longer, it would have been buried in the sand, not sitting on the surface like that. Look at it! It's still shiny black. Not a spot of rust.'

Reg didn't know what to say. He'd been exposed. All their dots, as DC Palumbo had called them, pointed to him, but how had they known to suspect him in the first place so they'd go looking for the evidence they'd found? How had he slipped up? 'What made you think it was me?'

'By assuming the person who killed Grace Williams knew her nosy neighbour would be away that day and had a reason for wanting to know that,' said DC Palumbo. 'Your name came up in conversation when we talked to some of her neighbour's friends.'

'Oh. I thought I must have let something slip.'

'You did, but we only found it once we knew where to look.'

'Want to tell us why you killed them?' said DS Healy.

'I don't think you'd understand.'

'Reginald Hartwood,' said DS Healy, 'I'm arresting you for the murders of Alastair Holt, Grace Williams, and Phil Snowdon.'

CHAPTER 35

IT WAS LATE, so after securing her evidence folder and laptop in her city office, Lina headed home. Celebrating the end of the investigation would have to wait. Besides, she had to be back in the office to brief the Police Prosecutor first thing in the morning, in preparation for Hartwood's appearance in court later in the day.

She thought she'd feel elated at cracking the case and hearing Hartwood confess, but she felt flat. Working with Tim was okay, but he wasn't Pat. She wanted to celebrate with Pat, but that was no longer possible. She missed his energy and sense of humour, and his fatherly interest in her career. She'd learnt a lot from him and his insistence on following the evidence, even when it didn't align with your current hypothesis.

She'd been lucky this time. The evidence had aligned with her hypothesis about the significance of Heather Fountain being away on the day Grace Williams had been murdered. Pat would have been proud of her and told everyone how she'd cracked the case. He'd have wanted people to know how good she was.

She smiled at the thought, but realised Tim's quieter approach would probably spare her from some of the unnecessary attention Pat's championing tended to attract.

When she got home, she allowed herself a glass of champagne to acknowledge her achievement. Then, she had a quick shower, before climbing into bed with the alarm set for seven, hoping that would give her enough time to prepare for their meeting with the Police Prosecutor at nine.

'What was that?' Lina was instantly alert. There it was again. Loud voices. Something was going on in the usually silent street outside. She glanced at the alarm clock. It was four-seventeen. She'd only been in bed for a couple of hours.

Annoyed, she grabbed her phone, slid out of bed and crossed to the window. She stood near the edge of the window and peered out into the street below through the gap between the curtain and the wall. In the moonlight, she could see two young men on the footpath opposite her apartment, fighting.

One was dressed in black, the other in shorts and a T-shirt, without shoes. Lights were coming on in windows in the surrounding houses. The one in the shorts fell backwards, clutching at his belly. The other turned and ran to the left, out of Lina's field of view. She rushed downstairs and threw open her front door, just in time to see a car without lights fly past at speed.

People were coming out into the street. She crossed to the youth lying on the footpath. His hands and T-shirt were covered in blood.

'Help me!'

'Stay calm! I'll call an ambulance.'

A woman she recognised from the local supermarket appeared out of the driveway of the house.

'Get a towel or something and see if you can staunch the bleeding! I'm calling an ambulance.'

'Shouldn't you be calling the police?' said a male voice.

'I am the police,' said Lina, pressing triple zero on her phone and giving the details to the operator before asking her to send both an ambulance and the police.

When she ended the call, there were two women attending to the young man on the footpath and several men standing around. Lina felt exposed in her knickers and T-shirt, but at least everybody else was in similar attire.

'Anyone get a good look at that car?'

'It's my dad's BMW,' said the young man at her feet. 'They were trying to steal it.'

Lina looked at him closely. He was the kid that lived three houses up the street. She wished she'd introduced herself to more of her neighbours. She knelt down next to him. 'Where's your dad?'

'In Melbourne.'

Thank God, thought Lina. 'What's your name?'

'Byron Withers.'

'Take it easy, Byron. The ambulance will be here soon.'

Lina stood and activated the torch on her phone before scanning the ground around where the fight had taken place. It didn't take her long to spot the knife the assailant had dropped in his haste to flee after having stabbed Byron.

'Please stay away from this part of the footpath, folks,' said Lina, pointing to where the knife lay. 'We don't want to contaminate that.'

'I didn't know you were a police officer,' said a man Lina

recognised as a person she sometimes caught the tram with. 'Paul Roberts. I live over there.' He pointed to the house next to Lina's apartment building.

'Lina Palumbo, I'm a detective, actually. That's why I don't wear a uniform.'

'I'm not complaining,' said Paul with a smile.

Cheeky bugger, thought Lina, but before she could respond, they were engulfed in flashing red and blue lights as an ambulance and a patrol car converged on them from opposite ends of the street. Lina went to converse with the patrol officers and pointed out the position of the knife the assailant had discarded.

Once the ambulance had departed with Byron, the group that had come out to investigate gathered in Lina's front room to give their initial statements to the attending officers before heading back to their beds.

Lina overheard Paul Roberts say he worked at Uni SA in the city as he was making his statement, and wondered what sort of work he did there. He was the last one to leave.

'Perhaps we could catch up some time, Lina, when we're more appropriately dressed.'

Lina liked the look of him in his boxer shorts and T-shirt, vulnerable and not at all threatening. 'That'd be nice, but don't feel as though you need to dress up for the occasion.'

He smiled. 'What are you doing tonight?'

'What have you got in mind?'

'How about we go for a drink on Jetty Road after work? I get home around six.'

'I should be here by then. Want to give me your number in case I get delayed?'

Lina looked at the alarm clock. It was five-twenty. She got back into bed but, with the adrenalin rush of the incident in the street and its surprise aftermath, couldn't go back to sleep. She could hardly believe someone had chatted her up at a crime scene and she'd taken a liking to him as soon as he'd smiled at her. What was even funnier was the fact that he lived next door, and they'd hardly spoken to each other in the three years since she'd moved into the apartment. Maybe there was a God after all, one with a sense of humour and good timing.

By seven, she was on the road heading into the office, hoping she'd be alert enough to get through the briefing with the Police Prosecutor.

CHAPTER 36

MARIANNE OPENED the door and was surprised to see DC Palumbo standing on the porch.

'Oh, hello. I wasn't expecting you.'

'Hello, Mrs Holt. There have been a few developments. May I come in?'

Marianne had heard about Reg being arrested over a hit-and-run accident on Seaford Road, which seemed so out of character for the Reg she knew, and wondered what else had happened. 'Let's go through to the back. Thomas is out there watering the garden.'

She closed the door and ushered DC Palumbo through the house to the alfresco area Alastair had been so keen on. 'Thomas, look who's here!'

'Hi, Lina! What brings you here?'

'I need to give you an update.'

'You could have called to do that, instead of dragging yourself all the way down here.'

'This is not one of those routine updates, Tom. We've made an arrest.'

Marianne pulled out a chair and sat down. 'Who?'

'Reg Hartwood.'

'Reg? You're not serious, are you?'

'He's confessed to killing Alastair and Grace, and Phil Snowdon.'

Reg? Marianne couldn't believe it. 'But Reg and Alastair were best mates?'

'Why?' said Thomas. 'Why would he do something like that?'

'He's not saying, but I think it's all connected to the affair Alastair was having with Grace.'

'What makes you say that?' said Thomas.

'Reg paid Phil Snowdon to install that surveillance camera in the ceiling fan in Grace's bedroom.'

'That doesn't sound like Reg,' said Marianne. 'Why would he do that?'

'Apparently, he became suspicious of Alastair's weekly pastoral care visits to Grace.'

'Dad did lots of regular pastoral care visits. I wondered what triggered his suspicions? Of course, we know now he was right to be suspicious, but how did he find out?'

'I gather it was something Grace's neighbour said to his sister-in-law. But we know Reg asked Phil to install the camera because we found a copy of the recording Phil made in Grace's bedroom on his computer.'

'If this Snowdon fellow was helping him, why did Reg kill him?' said Marianne, thinking none of this made any sense.

'Phil was blackmailing him.'

'This is going to be a disaster for the Community,' said Thomas. 'When's this going to be made public?'

DC Palumbo looked at her watch. 'There's a media briefing at noon. He's due in court this afternoon.'

'Is that why you're here?'

'I wanted you to hear it from me before it hits the news.'

'What happens now?' said Thomas.

'Well, if Reg goes ahead and pleads guilty, as he says he will, he'll be remanded in custody to await sentencing.'

'And if he changes his mind and pleads not guilty?' said Marianne. 'He likes a good argument.'

'Then, he'll be remanded in custody to await trial, and we'll have to present our evidence in court to show that he committed the murders.'

'I hope he doesn't do that, said Marianne. 'Having to go through all that again in public would be embarrassing.'

DC Palumbo squeezed her hand. 'I'll think he's going to plead guilty.'

'What about the hit-and-run?' said Thomas. 'We heard he'd been arrested for that.'

'He's confessed to that too,' said Lina, 'and the cyclist he hit has identified him as the driver of the vehicle.'

'Do you want to watch the midday news, Mum?'

'No, I think I'll have a cuppa.' Marianne turned to DC Palumbo. 'Got time to have one with us?'

Marianne sat in her favourite chair and gazed out at the back garden. She'd watched last night's evening news with Thomas after DC Palumbo had been. Reg had kept his word and pleaded guilty. Now, everyone in the Community knew what DC Palumbo had told them.

She'd spent the morning with her sister, rehashing the details and celebrating, in a way, that it was over, and she wouldn't have to sit through a court case and hear all the sordid details aired in public again.

She took a sip of her wine and glanced at their wedding photograph on the opposite wall. Her life had been turned upside down by a barbaric act committed by one of Alastair's best friends. She still didn't know whether she should be grateful for what Reg had done or angry. She was certainly sad for Megan and young Sophie. But she felt no sadness for herself.

On the contrary, despite what she'd told herself a good wife should feel, she was feeling relieved that Alastair was no longer part of her life. She wasn't happy he'd been murdered. No-one deserved that, no matter what they'd done. But she was glad he was no longer there telling her what to do and how to behave, and to mind her own business whenever she asked about anything to do with the church. It was liberating being in the house and not having to worry about pleasing him or crossing any of his red lines.

She was grateful he'd bought the house for them to retire in and left her with more than enough money to live on, even though in death he'd made a fool of her. She knew people felt sorry for her. They'd told her as much, but she no longer felt sorry for herself or cared what anyone else thought about her.

For the first time in a long time, she felt she was her own person again, and several of her friends had commented on how she'd come out of herself since Alastair's death. It was as if the girl she'd been before she'd married Alastair had been resurrected, and come back from the living death of her stifling marriage. Maybe that was what Jesus had meant about being born again? It certainly made more sense to her than what Alastair had told her it meant.

Marianne took another sip of wine and thought about Reg. She couldn't for the life of her understand why he'd done what he'd done. What was it to him if Alastair had been having an affair, she wondered. Had he been jealous or something?

She'd heard all the stories of how he and Alastair had chased the same girls at school, and she knew Reg was one of those blokes who always had to be top dog, to have the last say, which was why he'd been Chairman of the Council of Elders for so long. She wondered what would happen to the Council of Elders without him. She laughed. They'd probably be lost until someone else stepped in and took charge.

Maybe with new blood they'd finally come into the twenty-first century. They might even come to their senses and ask Thomas to resume his duties as their pastor. He'd had plenty of calls from Community members telling him they were petitioning the elders to reconsider his termination.

With Reg out of the picture, maybe they'd see the error of their ways. No-one, it seemed, liked the new guy. Not even Marianne, who thought he sounded like a clone of Alastair, and she'd heard more than enough preaching about hell and eternal damnation. She wondered how Alastair was finding the fires of hell he'd been so fond of describing. She shuddered at the thought and hoped Thomas was right about there being no such place.

It was getting late. Thomas had gone to help Sam do something. She looked at the clock on the wall. He'd be back soon, wanting something for dinner. She got up from her chair and headed into the kitchen, wondering if Sam's call had been a ruse to get Thomas alone so he could talk to him about coming back. She told herself she'd find out soon enough.

CHAPTER 37

ALTHOUGH THE ACTIVE phase of the investigation was over, Lina was still at her desk in the incident room at Christies Beach. The rest of the team, pulled into developing investigations, had already packed up and returned to Adelaide. Lina, however, had scored the task of winding up the investigation and curating the evidence they'd gathered for the Public Prosecutors to use in their sentencing submission.

It was a task that usually fell to the Senior Investigating Officer, but Tim had delegated it to her, arguing that since she'd been on the case from the start, she was in a better position to write it up than he was. Lina wasn't convinced, but she knew better than to object.

She'd written up cases before under Pat's guidance and knew what was required. It was a tedious task, but Pat had impressed on her the importance of doing it properly. A poorly written up case, he'd told her, failed the victim and the people who had worked on it, and it risked allowing the perpetrator's lawyers an opening to dismantle everything they'd worked to prove.

At least in this case, the perpetrator had decided to plead

guilty, which meant she had to make sure their evidence supported that claim, in case it turned out that Reg had covered for somebody else. That meant making sure they hadn't missed anything that his lawyer could claim pointed to another possible suspect or use as a mitigating circumstance.

The upside of writing up the case was a stretch of working regular hours, and knowing she wouldn't be called into another investigation until she'd handed over her report to the Public Prosecutors.

The incident room was quiet after the noise of a team working on an active investigation. The room still held the detritus of the case. Displays on the walls where they'd tried to map out and join their pieces of evidence and link them to their suspects. There were archive boxes holding paper copies of signed statements and plastic bags holding items collected from crime scenes. It was Lina's job to make sure they were all appropriately labelled and cross-referenced to her report and then placed into secure storage until they were needed.

Fortunately, the witness statements also existed in a digital format, as did the notes taken by investigating officers, along with the recordings and transcripts of interviews. The scene of crime reports and the pathologist's reports were also digital, which made it easier to package up the case into a digital format she could give to the Public Prosecutors.

DI Smith had advised her she'd be joining Tim Healy's team, at Tim's request, when she'd completed the case write up. Lina took that as a sign that, after all the pushback she'd experienced since she'd made the move out of Uniform, she'd finally made the grade as a detective in the eyes of her colleagues.

Lina gazed out into the blue sky, wondering where Pat was and whether he was happy. She missed him, and she knew Angela missed him. It appeared the rest of the world, though, had simply moved on as if he'd never existed. It felt a little strange reading his case notes and listening to his voice when she watched the recordings of an interview, knowing he was no longer there. Even though hearing his voice brought tears to her eyes, she was grateful for the memories those moments brought into her awareness.

She hoped he'd be proud of the detective he'd helped her become.

Lina answered her doorbell. Paul Roberts stood fully clothed on her entrance porch. Still good looking, she thought.

'Shall we catch the tram or do you want to walk?'

'Let's walk,' said Lina. 'It's not that far and I've been sitting down all day. Besides, it's a nice evening for a stroll.'

Paul smiled and moved back away from the doorway.

Lina felt her heart melt at his smile and stepped onto the porch so she could close the door. 'How long have you lived next door?'

'All my life, actually. It's my mother's house.'

They started walking towards Jetty Road.

'So, you live with you mum, then?'

'No, she remarried a couple of years back. They live on the Esplanade. How long have you lived down here?'

'Around three years. I bought this place when I became a detective.'

'I've seen you around,' said Paul. 'Always wondered what you did.'

Shy type, thought Lina, wondering where he'd found the courage to ask her out that morning. 'Why didn't you say hello before?'

'You always looked so professional and serious. I didn't think you'd notice someone like me.'

Lina smiled. 'Men have told me they find me intimidating. What made you change your mind?'

'Seeing you this morning, and I don't mean just seeing you in a T-shirt.' He blushed. 'Although that was nice, but seeing you as a vulnerable human being with a heart. The way you spoke to Byron.' He smiled again. 'I decided I wanted to get to know you.'

Lina stopped walking and turned to face him. 'That's got to be the nicest thing anybody has ever said to me.'

Paul blushed again.

It was obvious to Lina he didn't know what to say or do next. She touched his shoulder, and then stepped back and smiled. 'Shall we go and have this drink?'

A NOTE FROM PETER

If you enjoyed **Damnation,** you can help other readers share your enjoyment by telling them about the book and writing a review.

Drop by at **www.petermulraney.com** and join my **Crime Readers Group** to download a free copy of **Deadly Sands,** and be one of the first to know when my next book will be released.

Stella Bruno Investigates: Books 1 to 6

The Identity Thief Collection

The Fallout Collection

The Deception Collection

Ryan Holiday PI Short Stories

Rosie

Framed

Novella

The New Girlfriend

Living Alone series

After She's Gone

Cooking 4 One

Sanity Savers

Living Alone (Collection)

Living Alone Journal

Everyday Business Skills

Everyday Project Management

Everyday Productivity

Everyday Money Management

Writings of the Mystic

Sharing the Journey: Reflections of a Reluctant Mystic

My Life is My Responsibility: Insights for Conscious Living

I Am Affirmations: The Power of Words

Beyond the Words: Reflections on I Am Affirmations

Mystical Journey: A Handbook for Modern Mystics

Sharing the Journey Coloring Books

Mandalas

Mandalas by 3

Sharing the Journey Coloring Journals

Sharing the Journey Coloring Journal

Sharing the Journey Coloring Journal ∼Discovery

Sharing the Journey Coloring Journal ∼ Reflection